FRIGHT WATCH
UNMASKED

FRIGHT WATCH UNMASKED

LORIEN LAWRENCE

Amulet Books
New York

Cataloging-in-Publication Data has been applied for and may be obtained from the Library of Congress.

ISBN 978-1-4197-5929-1

Text © 2022 Lorien Lawrence
Illustrations by Kelley McMorris
Title lettering by David Coulson
Book design by Jade Rector and Brann Garvey

Published in 2022 by Amulet Books, an imprint of ABRAMS. All rights reserved. No portion of this book may be reproduced, stored in a retrieval system, or transmitted in any form or by any means, mechanical, electronic, photocopying, recording, or otherwise, without written permission from the publisher.

Printed and bound in U.S.A.
10 9 8 7 6 5 4 3 2 1

Amulet Books are available at special discounts when purchased in quantity for premiums and promotions as well as fundraising or educational use. Special editions can also be created to specification. For details, contact specialsales@abramsbooks.com or the address below.

Amulet Books® is a registered trademark of Harry N. Abrams, Inc.

ABRAMS The Art of Books
195 Broadway, New York, NY 10007
abramsbooks.com

For my mom

CHAPTER 1

I'm still having trouble with the nose.

Forget about fangs and claws, scales or fur—*noses* are the most terrifying part of making monsters. Every. Artist's. Nightmare. I mean, they seem simple—two nostrils and a beak—but realistic ones are nearly impossible to get right, and they're the first thing that people notice when an artist gets it wrong.

And I know a thing or two about getting it wrong. I tried at least ten versions before settling on this collapsed and sunken-in piece. It's a step in the right direction—at least it's starting to look more reptilian and swamp-like, with the nostrils more blended into the cheeks. Before my final sculpt, I'd tried more human-looking noses, with bridges slightly raised up away from the sharp cheekbones, but they just hadn't fit.

"He looks sad," Mom told me last week, before I'd even finished the molding. *"You sculpted his eyes down."*

"I thought it would make him look more human."

Mom chewed on the edge of a small raking tool, before driving it into the clay. *"The edges are too strong,"* she said, running her expert hands over the form. *"Soften them a bit. He needs to look like he's from the sea, not the moon."*

Together, we moved to reshape the creature's head, reworking the clay with our thumbs and pointer fingers, pressing and smoothing until the shapes started to take form into something—or someone—with a face: jutted cheekbones, elongated lips, flat nose, gills. Lots and lots of gills, starting at the cowl and building up toward the forehead and the top fin.

The creature looked menacing before the mold was cast, and now that I have the prosthetic nuzzled against the foam model head, Winston, my latest creation, looks even more so.

I step back and squint through my cat's-eye glasses at the creature's nose. *Still kind of wonky.* I mean, it's definitely better, but I'm not going for *better*: I'm going for perfect.

"Right now, you're not cutting it," I say, grabbing my airbrush. "Maybe I can fix you with the paint."

I begin to spray a thin layer of shimmer in circular motions around Winston's face, starting with the center. Mom was right: the metallic sheen definitely pops over the base coats of true green and lime that she had recommended.

"You need a bit of sparkle, honey, or else the greens will look muddy and none of the features will read from far away. You want people to notice the little things. Every. Single. Gill."

My mom knows what she's talking about. She's a makeup artist at a big cosmetic chain store. She used to dream of working on movie sets, but then she got pregnant and has been at the mall ever since. Sometimes I feel kind of guilty about it, but she seems happy enough to be stuck with Dad, my older sister, Margot, and me.

"I'm not so bad, am I, Winston?"

With each gentle hiss my gun makes, with each spray, with each layer, Winston begins to wake up, staring out at me with his hollow eyes. It's starting to feel as if I'm looking at a real sea monster, something that—like any good makeup—feels real enough to reach out and touch you. Or grab you and pull you down beneath the surface.

"You're getting better," I tell him, my fingers tingling as I work, the rhythmic hiss of the gun filling the space in the room.

But the nose . . . The nose . . . It still doesn't look right. *What if?*

I load a sky-blue canister into my airbrush and spray a few test puffs onto my arm. *This might just work.*

Carefully, I raise the gun to the center of Winston's face and gently spray dots of crisp blue along the sides of each nostril.

"Marion!" Mom calls from downstairs.

I ignore her and keep painting, my eyes refusing to blink as I hold my breath. Almost there . . .

Mom's voice cuts down an octave. "Come on, birthday girl. Before your dad eats all the cake!"

I instantly drop my airbrush; it falls with a loud clank against the metal counter.

"She's not messing around," Dad calls up. "I have zero self-control when it comes to baked goods."

"Quick, Mar, he's trying to steal the frosting!"

"Coming!" I call back.

I switch off the overhead light and slip past the divider into the bedroom part of my room.

Last year, Dad built me a temporary wall to separate my bed from my workshop. So, now, I don't have to have my makeup supplies balanced on top of my schoolbooks, or monster faces staring at me while I sleep. However, I do still have a few framed monster movie posters in my bedroom—mostly stuff from the 1980s, my most favorite monster era of all time. Mom even helped me make custom gold frames to hang against my robin's-egg-colored walls to make them really pop. Kids at school are usually surprised to see what my room looks like when they come over for Halloween makeups. Maybe they expect it to be painted all black with a bed in the shape of a coffin or something. Truth is, I love color. I *respect* color. I just don't wear color. Well, not much of it anyway—just a pop of lavender in my glasses, and my new emerald-green Doc Martens that I got this morning as a present.

Most fourteen-year-olds have parties on their birthdays, but I don't really have people I'm close to. So, instead of taking up a table at Cucina Della Nonna or Harvey's and gorging on pizza and milkshakes with a few kids from school, I have a quiet night planned here at home.

I make my way downstairs, careful not to mess up the fake cobwebs tied to the banister.

Our whole house is decked out for Halloween: pumpkins, witches, ghosts, not to mention skulls—*so* many skulls. Mom kind of has a thing for skeletons, and we have them displayed on nearly every surface in nearly every color, leaning against vintage-looking spell jars and tapered black candles that smell like pumpkin spice. Right now, she's even wearing a dress patterned in bones. She beams at me from the bottom of the stairs, her makeup immaculate, her black hair falling over her shoulders in neat waves.

"Happy birthday!" she cries.

"Happy birthday!" Dad and Margot chime in.

"Thanks," I say, suddenly shy, even though I have no reason to be.

They pull me in for a tight group hug, and then Dad leads me over to the coffee table where the birthday cake is waiting.

"So, I get the first piece, right?" he teases.

"You wish," I tell him.

Mom carefully passes me a knife. "*Marion* gets the first piece," she says.

Dad pretends to pout, and my sister nudges him in the ribs.

The cake is everything. It's shaped like a bat, covered in purple fondant, with dark chocolate eyes and candy corn teeth. When I cut through the middle, the insides bleed red velvet and marshmallow buttercream—my favorite. I tilt a giant slice onto my plate.

"Eat up, eat up," Mom tells us.

We dig in, and the cake is so rich and moist that it literally melts in my mouth. Mom gets her own plate and snuggles up beside me on the couch. Dad sits on my other side, leaving Margot with the oversized armchair.

"So, *Cujo*, right?" Dad asks, pretending to cue up the classic Stephen King film.

"*Young Frankenstein*," I tell him.

He sighs heavily, pretending to be upset, but I see the

smile on his face as he flips through the streaming movies. *Young Frankenstein* is a tradition—we've been watching it on my birthday since I was little.

Watching it feels so cozy and familiar. Even Margot laughs along with the movie's jokes. By the time the credits roll, we've succeeded in our mission to finish off the bat cake.

Mom pats the side of my knee before she stands. "Come on," she tells me, beckoning me to the kitchen. "A birthday reading for my birthday girl," she says with a smile.

I snap the rubber band against my wrist, before following her to the kitchen table. I watch quietly as Mom lights a candle that smells of lavender and sage, casting a dreamy spell over the room. She then sets a tin box onto the table, the cover of which is hand-painted in cerulean-blue swirls. From the box she pulls out a deck of tarot cards, and she hands it to me for shuffling. I close my eyes as I mix up the deck, cutting it three times before handing the cards back over to Mom. I can hear the low hum of the TV coming from the next room; Dad and Margot must have turned on another movie. They've never been into Mom's readings. Mom, for her part, has always claimed to be "a bit psychic," just like Grandma Goldie in California, and Goldie's mother before her, and so on. Magic supposedly runs in the family.

Goldie used to insist I'd discover my gift one day, too, but to be honest, I've always been on the fence about magic; after all, the most magical things I've ever seen were created with paint and clay, and they're meant to be illusions. Just art, not hocus-pocus.

Still, when I reopen my eyes, I have to admit that Mom looks pretty magical across the table. In the candlelight, her pale skin glows like fairy dust, and her dark eyes shine as if they hold a million different secrets. I watch her fan the cards across the table. She then sits back and rolls up the sleeves of her dress, the one she found last summer at the outdoor flea market. "Are you ready to know your future?"

"I guess."

"Pick your cards, honey."

My stomach does a little flip as I reach forward and lift ten cards, not looking at them as I choose. I drop them one at a time into Mom's hands as if each of them was made of fire. Mom moves the extra cards to the other side of the table before laying out my selection: the first six make a cross, while the last four create a column down the right-hand side. My knees bounce against the silence, and my fingers instinctively reach for the black rubber band around my wrist. I ping it against my skin, causing a mild stinging sensation, and exhale in time to the snaps—*three, two, one.*

Mom notices, arching an eyebrow. "Is this making you anxious? Because we don't have to—"

"I'm fine," I lie, snapping the rubber band one last time. My fingers tingle as I press them against the top of the table. "Let's do it."

Mom studies me for a moment, but I put on my best poker face, causing her to relent. She starts to read the cards, pointing to each one as she goes. Some of the faces look familiar, like the first one: the High Priestess, sitting on a throne while draped in white and blue robes.

"This card symbolizes your environment," Mom says, her voice rich like velvet, her movements stirring the candle's flame so that shapes and shadows dance along her skin. "You crave silence and privacy, and you use this to your advantage. You're *smart*, baby girl. So smart. But this"—she taps the black column in the picture—"shows the potential for mystery, for things unknown to filter in your life."

Her eyes widen with the same dramatic flair that I used to love as a kid. Tonight, though, I just wish that she would hurry up. I don't like my secrets spread out across the table, exposing my many flaws.

"Next?" I ask quietly, as my knee starts bouncing again.

Mom points to the second card. "This represents your obstacles, or things you're trying to overcome. And you drew the Moon, which symbolizes anxiety." She lets the last word hover in the air, its familiarity weighing on my chest. She reaches out to touch my cheek before moving on to the next card.

"This represents the best version of yourself, or the type of person you want to be," she says, pointing to the card with two swords crossing over a blindfolded person's chest. Behind the man is a calm-looking sea. "Friendship, cooperation—wanting to be part of a group."

I lean forward and gesture to the next set of cards: the Star, the Ace of Wands, and the upside-down Five of Wands. "What about these ones?" I ask. "What do these mean?"

Mom purses her red-painted lips as she considers the trio. "Your strength is your creativity." She smiles. "Which we already knew, my little artist." She points to the sixth card. "But *this* shows that trickery is on its way, so you have to be cautious. You have to keep your eyes and ears open."

I skim over the last column, recognizing a few of the cards and what they symbolize: fear, anxiety, loneliness. However, the last card is the one that catches my eye, with its depiction of a skeleton wearing a knight's armor, riding on a white horse and carrying a flag printed with a five-petal rose. Death. I point to it, my finger shaking.

Mom waves me away. "Oh, don't worry, Marion. The Death card doesn't mean *death* death. It means that change is coming—some kind of transformation." She takes my hand and squeezes. "It can mean *rebirth*, my birthday girl."

Mom's reading stays with me through the rest of the night, the skeletal soldier haunting my dreams. I toss and turn for hours, snapping my rubber band, until around five in the morning when I finally give up on sleep. Throwing the covers off me, I stumble through the dark toward my workshop. Here, I turn on the overhead light, squinting until my eyes adjust to the brightness.

Winston is the first thing I see, and his image is instantly soothing. Last night, I tried to come up with ways to fix his nose with paint. Now, I take a seat on my stool and try to remember the ideas.

What if I outline the edges in black? *No—too drastic.*

What if I add a bit more shimmer? *No—too amateur. I don't want him to look like a glitter bomb . . .*

I tap my pencil against the counter as I study the mask, noting how the curved lines highlight the narrow cheekbones and pointy chin. Thank goodness the fan of gills turned out OK; that was the most tedious part, so far. I spent hours watching videos of fish until I figured out their anatomy, like how they move and breathe. The sculpture itself took two days to finish. I guess it paid off, though, because the gills look real enough to move by themselves. For a moment, they actually do—their edges fluttering as if in water.

I must be really *tired,* I think, rubbing my eyes.

When I refocus, Winston looks totally normal. I shrug it off and load up the airbrush, getting to work. First, I add a touch of violet to the cheekbones, enhancing their inhuman shape. Then I swap that color out for a light cerulean, which I shade along the forehead, swooping along the gill line. Finally, I move over to the nose, forming tiny dots and ridges, providing some much-needed texture to the surface.

"Marion, come down for breakfast!" Mom suddenly calls, startling me.

My eyes shift toward the clock on my phone. It's already six thirty! I must have lost track of time.

Quickly, I scrub my hands with a Wet One before throwing one last glance over to Winston: the blue highlights are working—the nose is finally starting to take shape! I wish that I could just stay and finish it up, but Mrs. Davis will have a meltdown if I'm late for homeroom again.

"Marion!" Mom's voice cuts through my thoughts.

"Coming!" I yell back.

I tug on my favorite black dress and my new boots, then twist my dark hair into a knot on the top of my head, before flying down the stairs.

My parents shoot me a look as I come into the kitchen. They balance pieces of toast against full mugs of coffee.

"Wash your hands," Mom says, eyeing the blue streaks on my arm.

"I wiped them already."

"Not the same. Wash."

I sigh and quickly scrub my hands under the sink. When I'm finished, Dad extends a mug and a plate toward me.

"Thanks." I gratefully accept the mug and dip my face into the steam, inhaling the rich, hazelnut scent. If this were a movie, the dad character would make an unfunny joke about how I was too young to be this tired, swapping my mug for a glass of orange juice. I silently thank the universe for giving me two parents who don't mind their teenager sucking down coffee every morning.

"How's Winston?" Mom asks.

I grin through a bite of toast. "I added blue around the nose."

"Brilliant! Man, why didn't I think of that?"

"I don't know. I'm not done yet, but it's definitely helping."

Dad raises an eyebrow. "I don't get it. How can the color blue help a nose?" He shakes his head before Mom or I can answer. "Never mind. We probably don't have time for you to explain it to me."

"It's OK, honey," Mom says with a smile, "we can't all be creative geniuses."

Dad makes a face as he drains his coffee, dropping the empty mug onto the table with a thud. "So, what's on the docket this year? How many clients we looking at?"

"Twenty."

He whistles. "That seems like a lot, doesn't it? Double from last year. You sure you can get it all done in time for the dance?"

"Thanks for the vote of confidence, Dad."

"I just meant—"

I wave him off with the crust of my toast. "Don't worry.

I have it all under control. I started making the prosthetic pieces months ago, so all I have to do is apply and paint. And Mom's helping me."

"That I am," Mom says, standing up and dropping our plates in the sink. She straightens the boldly patterned skirt that hugs her curves and slips into a pair of chunky heels. Her black hair spills down her back, grazing her colorful sleeve tattoos.

Both of my parents' arms are covered in ink, something that looks and feels totally natural in our house, as if they were born like that. I'm already counting down the years until I can make my own mark. I even have my first tattoo picked out: a black-and-white portrait of the Wolf Man, the first on-screen werewolf. Sometimes I draw it myself with a Sharpie on the inside of my left arm. But Mom says I have to wait until I'm eighteen for the real thing.

"Where's your sister? We're going to be late." Dad says, looking around. "*Margot!*"

"Relax, I'm right here," Margot says, suddenly appearing in the kitchen. Like Mom, Margot favors the whole vintage look, except Margot is more Nancy Drew than rockabilly. Right now, she's wearing a plaid skirt with knee-high socks, her raven hair held back with a velvet headband. On her wrist is a simple watch—no rubber band. She doesn't need it like I do.

"Nice boots, Marion," she says to me.

"Thanks." I smile. Compliments from Margot are a rare thing.

"Margot, have something for breakfast," Mom tells her.

Margot grabs an apple from the bowl before opening her leather backpack and pulling out a book. "Finished it last night," she says, handing the book to Dad. "It was OK."

Dad frowns at her. "Just *OK*?"

Margot shrugs one shoulder. "It got kind of repetitive toward the end."

"It was supposed to be repetitive—it's metaphorical!"

She bites a large chunk out of her apple. "Metaphorical for *what*?"

Dad and Margot have this unofficial book club between them. They swap books and argue about them on the regular: Margot trading her Gothic horrors and literary fictions for Dad's punk rock memoirs.

"You two can argue about it later," Mom interrupts, slipping into her scarlet peacoat. "It's time to go. Come on, Margot."

Margot closes her backpack and swings it over her shoulders, before throwing out a general *goodbye* to the room and making her way out the door.

Mom leans over to kiss me on the head, and I rub a napkin against my skin to wipe off the smear of red lipstick she inevitably leaves behind. "Have a good day at school, honey." She then exits in a breeze of orange spice perfume.

"Finish up, kiddo," Dad says while tugging on his work boots. "You've got school, and I've got a garage full of cars to fix." He stands up and grabs his keys from off the counter.

The word *school* sucks all the magic out of the air, making me feel cold and stiff. I drain the last of my now-lukewarm coffee, before reluctantly grabbing my backpack and my lunch box: the metal one with Count Chocula's face printed across the front.

"The boots look good," Dad tells me with a grin. "I still can't believe my baby's fourteen."

I roll my eyes and gently push past him. "Don't get all sappy, Dad. Come on."

With this, he follows me out to his pickup truck, which is so high off the ground that he had to install an extra step just for the rest of us to get in.

"Seat belt," he tells me inside.

I pull the strap across my chest. "As if I would forget."

Dad fires up the ignition, and his loud punk music fills the cabin. I crack my window just to release a bit of the sound. Dad drums his thumbs against the steering wheel as he backs out of the driveway. For a few minutes, we bop our heads in time to the beat as we ease down a collection of side streets and neat, two-story homes, past a cluster of trees with red and golden leaves.

Dad lowers the music. "So . . ."

I side-eye him. "So?"

"What are you planning to wear to the dance? Did you make yourself a mask? Is that what Winston's for?"

I shift against the worn leather. "Winston's for my portfolio, Dad. I'm not going to wear him."

"Then what are you going to be?"

I shrug. "Nothing."

"Nothing? Why? You need suggestions? What about Cujo? I bet you'd do a great Cujo makeup."

"Cujo as in the rabid dog?

Dad blinks. "Is there any other?"

"You're obsessed with Stephen King."

"Because he's the *king* of horror." He winks at me. "Get it? *King*?"

I roll my eyes. "Yes, Dad, I get it. But I'm not going to be Cujo for Halloween."

He shrugs. "Then what about Beetlejuice?"

"No."

"Annabelle?"

"Nope."

"Really? But you do the creepy doll makeup so well . . ."

"Dad, I don't need suggestions because I don't need a costume. I'm not going to the dance."

He looks at me briefly before slamming on the brakes as we come to a stop sign. "That's ridiculous, Marion. Why wouldn't you want to go to the dance?" He puts his foot back on the gas a bit too hard, jutting us both forward.

I turn to the window, watching the colors whip by through the glass. "Dances are stupid," I mumble, clutching my lunch box tighter in my hands.

"Dances are a rite of passage."

"Who cares?"

"I mean, come on, honey, you work so hard. Don't you want to at least see all of your monsters out there in the wild?"

"Not really," I lie, pinging the rubber band against my wrist: *four ... three ... two ...*

We pull up to the front of Rocky Hill Middle School, and never have I ever been more excited to see this old stack of bricks.

"Thanks for the ride," I say, quickly gathering my things.

Dad throws the truck into park. "Hey, I know you're fourteen now and everything, but that doesn't mean you can't give your old man a kiss on the cheek."

I bite my lip and look at him. "It kind of does, Dad."

He lets out an exaggerated sigh as the car behind us blares its horn; I guess we're taking too long.

"Fist bump, then?"

I smile at him and thrust out my fist. "Sure."

We gently pound each other's knuckles before I swing open the door, starting the long, slow march toward the building. Dad's music follows me until I reach the door.

CHAPTER 2

School feels different even before I turn down the familiar hallway; there's a buzz in the air, an energy. People actually seem excited as they scurry toward their lockers.

It must be the decorations. The normally drab walls are now littered with orange, black, and purple posters reminding us of the Halloween dance; they hang from fishing line like bats so that they flutter over our heads. Someone even went through the trouble of taping individual flyers to every single one of our lockers, and a discarded pile starts to build on the floor near the trash as students rip them down, laughing, making plans, and talking up the big night.

I gently lift the poster on my own locker, reading the details:

Come one, come all to the

ROCKY HILL HALLOWEEN DANCE!

Friday, October 31, 6–9 p.m.
Merrick's by the Sea Community Center
Tickets: $10 in advance or $15 at the door
Prizes for best costumes

"Looks like the student council went a little batty this year."

My entire body suddenly becomes boneless, as if the sound of his voice is somehow able to turn my vertebrae and patella into a mush of soppy goo. I spin around and come face-to-face with Tyler Dash.

He laughs at his own cheesy pun, his brown eyes crinkling around the edges. "Get it? *Batty*? 'Cause they look like bats?" He whacks one of the posters above his head, sending it whirling on the fishing line.

I try to laugh along with him, but it comes out in a loud snort instead of a cute giggle. I feel my cheeks start to burn just as the homeroom bell rings.

Tyler grins up at me from beneath his mess of chestnut curls. *Goofy*—that's how I've heard other girls describe him. But I don't see goofy. I just see his dimples, and a smile so wide that it seems to take up his entire face.

"See you in art," he tells me.

"Yeah. See you."

I watch him go, my cheeks still on fire. *Stupid snort,* I think, before trudging off to Mrs. Davis's class.

I'm ambushed before I can even sit down.

"Marion," Stella Naples calls, barreling toward me. "I have a question for you. Here, sit with me."

Stella and I slide into desks beside each other. I immediately uncap a Sharpie and begin doodling on the cover of my composition notebook. "What's up?" I ask without meeting her eyes.

But I already know what's up; I can tell what she's going to ask even before she opens her mouth.

"It's about the dance on Friday," she says, digging into her sparkly pencil case. She pulls out an unopened, share-size bag of Sour Patch Watermelon. My favorite. This girl did her homework. She extends it to me. "Want some?"

Yes. Yes, I do. "No, thanks. I just ate breakfast."

Stella bites her bottom lip and pushes the bag toward me. "Well, take them anyway. You might want them after lunch or something." She offers a weak, desperate smile.

"Thanks." My Docs tap impatiently against the tile floor as I wait for her to ask what she's inevitably going to ask.

"So, I got this costume," she starts.

Here it is . . .

"And it's super low-key. Just like your classic witch. But I was trying it on last night and was thinking it would look *so* much cooler if it had a pointy nose or something. You know, something more . . ." She searches for the word. "*Authentic?*"

I shake my head. "Sorry, Stella. I'm already booked up."

"I know, but this would be just like the teeniest, littlest thing. I'm sure it wouldn't take long. And it might even help me win one of the costume prizes."

"I can't, Stella."

"But what if I—"

"Look, there's no way that I can custom-make a nose for you in time for Friday. I booked up over the summer. I'm sorry." I push the Sour Patch across the desk. "Do you want these back?"

She shakes her head. "No. It's cool. You keep them."

Guilt sinks in. I do a mental inventory of my prosthetic stockpile at home. "Wait," I say, just as Stella's about to get up. "I might have an extra witch's nose lying around some-where. I can pre-paint it and sell it to you for ten bucks with the glue, but you'd have to apply it to yourself, and it might not fit you perfectly." I shrug. "That's the best I can offer."

Stella's face lights up. "Perfect, perfect, perfect! I mean, how hard can it be to glue a nose to my face?" She rolls her eyes for emphasis, and it takes everything in me not to roll mine back: she's a client, after all, and I have to be nice.

"OK. You can pick it up on Friday at three. I'll give you the glue and the instructions in a bag. Just make sure you follow the directions."

Stella waves a hand at me as the bell rings. "Yeah, of course. Thanks so much, Marion. You're, like, the Queen of Halloween or something!"

"Yeah," I mutter, "or something."

I stuff the bag of candy into my pencil case while Mrs. Davis takes attendance. Then I make my way to first period, language arts.

I usually prefer movies to books, but Mr. Dupois makes it fun enough, especially this week: we're studying urban legends and folklore. The creepier the better, as far as I'm concerned. I'm partial to the folklore, because of the monsters and mystical creatures. But the urban legends are way more messed up—I don't really like stories where people attack one another. Mom always says that the worst kinds of monsters are the human kind.

I don't dare bring this up to Mr. Dupois, though—I don't talk in class unless I'm forced to. Last year, one of my teachers, Mrs. McCabe, called Mom and Dad in for a parent-teacher conference about my lack of participation. She said that I was *unengaged* and that they *needed to get me out of my shell.* Like I was some kind of turtle or a cicada or something.

I was pretty sure that Mom filled Mrs. McCabe in about my anxiety. She probably explained how I was still seeing Dr. Magesh, who has been my therapist since I was eight years old, when the attacks began. One day I was playing with LEGOs at my friend Lyndsay's house when all of a sudden I became really hot, and it felt as though a pair of heavy, imaginary hands were pressing against my chest. By the time Lyndsay's mom called my parents, I was struggling to catch my breath. My own panic had stained the room and everyone in it. My friend was scared—too scared to invite me over again.

"*She's broken,*" I'd overheard her tell our tablemates at lunch one day. "*She was lying on top of the LEGOs for like an hour, just making these squeaky sounds. It was like she couldn't breathe...*"

Lyndsay was right: I couldn't breathe. And for a few moments on that worn brown carpet, I'd felt the walls closing in on me, and I didn't think I'd ever get home.

"*Anxiety attack,*" Dr. Magesh explained. She went on to list the symptoms and the therapies. My black rubber band was her idea. "*Snap it when the symptoms start. Not too hard, but not too soft.*" It's kind of been a part of me ever since, like an extension of my wrist.

I snap it now, waiting for Mr. Dupois to start the class.

"Since we're going to start discussing community storytelling this week, tonight, for homework," he explains, "choose your favorite folktale or urban legend. Summarize it, reflect on it, and be ready to share it tomorrow with the class."

Great. Another teacher ruining a perfectly good assignment by adding a stupid share-out.

I go through the motions in my next three classes, where I count down the minutes until lunch. Not that I particularly love lunch—I don't. It's not my favorite period of the day. But I don't *dislike* it either. It just feels like a bit of a show, with everybody talking too loudly and trying too hard.

My usual table is tucked near the stairs in the back corner of the cafeteria. It's about as out of the way as you can get, and I've been eating here with a small group of Dungeons & Dragons players since the sixth grade. We're more like lunch friends, not real friends, especially since I don't role-play. I've said *no* to game nights so many times over the years that they've finally stopped inviting me. It's probably for the best. I don't want to rock the boat and go to a game night, only to have them get sick of me. I'm lucky they're still fine with me sitting with them.

Janae, the dragon leader—or Dungeon Master—waves to me from the pizza line. I wave back and head over to join the rest of the crew: Shannon the rogue shifter, Tanya the elvish cleric, Carter the leonin monk, and Eitan the kenku ranger. Even though I don't go to their games, I still know a lot about their campaign. Together, we make up *The*

Table of Misfit Toys, as I once overheard the French teacher, Madame Jean, refer to us.

"Ooh, check out the boots," Shannon says as I approach. Her eyes as are as green as my Docs, and they sparkle as I sit down beside her. "Birthday present?"

"Yup."

"What else did you get?" Janae asks, sliding in with her slice of pizza. She takes an oversized bite. "More makeup stuff?"

"Obviously," Shannon says, bobbing her head. "'Tis the season, right? I mean, did you see all of those flyers this morning? You must be making bank this weekend, Mar."

I open my container of hummus and carrots, nodding as I chew.

"How many clients you up to now?" Tanya asks, stealing the Sour Patch candies from my pencil case.

"Twenty. Well, twenty-one if you count Stella."

Tanya whistles and pushes the candy over to Carter; he silently takes a handful and continues reading his fantasy novel—Carter rarely talks. He's so quiet, in fact, that I struggle to picture him participating in any sort of role-playing game, but Shannon swears he comes alive whenever there are any dice around.

He passes my candy to Eitan beside him. Eitan furrows his sharp brows and pops one into his mouth. He chews thoughtfully for a moment before passing the now half-empty bag back to me. "You know," he starts, "I feel like there's a story here. With *you*."

I blink. "Me?"

Eitan nods, framing his hands in the air above an imaginary headline. "Teenage Monster Maker." He frowns. "Or something like that."

"Oh my gosh, that's such a great idea!" Janae squeals. "Eitan, you have to talk to Tyler."

My stomach dips at the mention of Tyler's name. "Tyler *Dash*?" I ask, even though I already know the answer. Tyler and Eitan are friends. Tyler would probably eat lunch with us if he ever came to the cafeteria; he eats with the rest of the school paper team in the Rocky Hill newsroom upstairs in Mr. Collier's class. The whole eating-lunch-on-the-job thing was the main reason why Eitan quit the paper, but he and Tyler are still close.

"I think Tyler would be into it," Eitan says. "He told me that they're working on the Halloween issue. He's going to be covering the dance."

"Oh, I'm not going to the dance."

Eitan shrugs. "Doesn't matter. You're doing makeups for it, aren't you?"

"Yeah, but—"

"Think about it, Marion," Shannon says dreamily. "It'd be so cool to have your own spread."

"Not to mention, it would probably be good for business," Tanya adds. "Isn't the winter play coming up? And then the spring dance? You can start taking orders, like, ASAP. I mean, seriously—if this goes well, you can start taking orders for *next* Halloween even."

I pick at my lunch, weighing each of their words. On the one hand, they're right: a story in the school paper *would* be good for business. On the other hand, it would involve actually talking to Tyler, and judging by this morning's snort-fest, that's easier said than done.

"Hey, Marion," Alexa Vega says, dropping down on the bench beside me and saving me from this discussion. She bats her eyes, the lashes of which are coated in a blue shimmer that seems to reflect the otherwise dull lighting in the cafeteria. Her entire outfit is dripping with color.

"Hey, Lex." I push away my lunch and offer her a professional smile. "What's up?" The other Misfit Toys watch us quietly with interest.

"I wanted to check in on our makeups for Friday," Lex says, flapping her hands as she talks. "Are we cool?"

I nod. "All of the prosthetics are made and pre-painted. So, I'll be able to apply them pretty quickly before the dance, and then just do the final touch-ups once they're on."

"What's your costume?" Shannon asks.

Lex's eyes sparkle. "We're going as the old people from Goodie Lane."

Shannon thinks for a minute, trying to place them. "Oh, you mean the weird ones? Ms. Bea and her neighbors?"

Lex grins proudly. "Yup."

Ms. Bea—Beatrice—and her friends were like a semi-famous group of senior citizens, until they mysteriously skipped town last summer. For as long as anyone could remember, they lived on Goodie Lane. Rumor has it that they were immortal or something—they never seemed to age. It's a pretty cool costume idea, but this will be my first old-age makeup, which is nerve-racking and exciting. I just hope more than anything that I'm able to deliver something authentic.

"What are you all going as?" Lex asks.

Janae answers for the group. "We're not going. We're having a big Halloween-themed game. It's kind of like tradition."

Lex nods. "Cool." She turns to me. "Hey, come to my table for a sec. I think Kaylee wanted to ask you something."

My limbs become heavy: I hate talking to new people. But this isn't a social visit—it's for business. So, I force a short nod and follow her across the cafeteria, snapping my rubber band with each step.

We approach the end of a long table, and Lex slides into a seat beside three other girls. I recognize them and know their names but have never spoken to any of them before. Two of the girls, Quinn and Kaylee, run on the school's track team, while Zoe, the blonde one, seems to live on her skateboard when she's not in school.

"Hey," they say in unison, offering small waves.

"Hey," I say back, still pinging my rubber band against my wrist.

"Kay, what did you want to ask her?" Lex says, nodding to the girl with the glasses.

"Oh yeah. Should I wash my face before the makeup?" Kaylee asks.

I nod, relaxing as the conversation steers toward my area of expertise. "That's probably a good idea." I look from face to face. "Who's going to be which person?"

"I'm Mrs. Brown," Lex says.

Kaylee raises her hand. "I'm Mrs. Smith."

"And I'm Ms. Attwood," Zoe says.

Which leaves Quinn, who hesitates before finally mumbling, "Bea."

I smile. Bea was the one who used to run a cosmetics boutique down by the beach. Mom and I went in there a few times, but Mom said all the products were overpriced, and she couldn't figure out what was in any of them. For her part, Bea was one of the most glamorous people in town, wearing silk evening gowns just to go grocery shopping.

Lex pouts. "It's not fair—I wanted to be Ms. Bea."

Quinn's face seems to darken. "Not on your life."

She gives off the vibe that *something* went down between her and Bea. I'm kind of curious, but I don't know Quinn well enough to ask questions.

Lex sighs dreamily. "But Bea has the most amazing style," she whines.

"Had. She *had* the most amazing style," Quinn shoots back.

"Quinn, she could have just moved," Zoe says, rolling her eyes. "Why do you always talk about her like she's dead?"

Suddenly this guy from my language arts class, Mike Warren, jumps out from behind me. "Boo!" he cries, causing Quinn to yelp before she promptly whacks him in the arm.

"What's wrong with you?" she cries.

Mike is laughing too hard to apologize. He swipes a fry from Quinn's plate before he notices me. "Oh, hey, you're the monster girl, right?"

"She's the monster *makeup* artist, not the monster girl," Lex corrects.

"Oh, my bad."

Quinn throws a fry at his face.

"What are you going as?" I ask. I study his athletic clothes, assuming he's going to say that he's dressing as a baseball player or something.

Mike shrugs. "Haven't thought about it yet. You're doing their makeup, right?"

"Yup," Lex answers for me. "When you see us on Friday, we'll be transformed into your old neighbors."

Mike stops smiling and exchanges a look with Quinn before asking, "Seriously, Parker?"

She just shrugs in response. I don't know why, but a tension fills the air.

I start backing up toward my table. "Guess I'll see you on Friday at my house. You have the address?"

Lex nods. "Thanks, Marion. We'll see you Friday!"

With this, I hurry back to the Misfit Toys, where I listen to my tablemates argue over whether Janae's newest dice are cursed.

My stomach flips when lunch ends, because next up is art class with Tyler Dash.

"See you later, Mar," Shannon and the rest of them call.

Tanya steals a few more Sour Patch candies before giggling and trotting off in the opposite direction. I take my time gathering my things; I don't like being in the crowded hallway after lunch. I guess I take a little too long, because I make it to art class a few seconds after the bell rings. Slinking in, I grab my collage from the table. Thankfully, Mrs. Anderson doesn't seem to notice, but Tyler does. He waves me over with one of his big smiles, and I smile back on command, praying that it's not too toothy or weird. I touch my hair to make sure it's still properly in place, before hopping onto a stool beside him.

"Late to class, huh?" he asks, nudging me in the arm. "My days."

I swoon a little bit in my seat. *My days.* No one else in town would say something like that. That's one of the things that I love about Tyler: his dad is British, so he sometimes says phrases that are from the UK. They're slightly offbeat and always adorable. Last week, I asked him what "my days" meant, and he laughed and explained that it was like saying "Oh my goodness." Now he seems to say it every time he sees me, kind of like it's our thing.

"I was *barely* late," I tell him.

Before he can respond, Mrs. Anderson calls me over. Tyler whistles under his breath, implying that I'm in trouble. My body tenses as I head up toward her desk at the front of the room.

"I'm sorry I'm late," I tell her, the words spilling out. "I was just—"

She shakes her head, cutting me off. "Relax, Marion. That's not what I want to talk to you about."

"It's not?"

"Nope." She smiles at me. "I was wondering if you've ever thought about doing the winter play?"

"Umm, I don't act," I tell her.

At this, she laughs lightly. "No, we don't want you to act, Marion. I was talking with the director, and he was wondering if you'd be interested in being the makeup artist for the actors? I know you usually help out individual kids who ask, but this year we were thinking it could be more official."

"Oh. Really?" I can't hide my shock.

Mrs. Anderson's smile grows. "Well, of course. You're Rocky Hill's special effects star. It seems fitting for you to be part of the theater. You don't have to answer right now. Just think about it. We have some time for you to decide."

No, I want to say. *For a million reasons, no.* Makeup is the one thing that makes me feel good about myself. What if I mess up the makeups for the play, and the whole school sees? Besides, if I do this for free, I won't get paid on the side. And I desperately want a new airbrush machine.

"Just let me know in a week or two," Mrs. Anderson continues. "But honestly, Marion, we'd be honored to have you."

I shift my weight. "What's the play going to be, anyway?"

"*Little Shop of Horrors.*" She grins. "We thought it'd be right up your alley." Then she starts to walk away toward a group of kids who just spilled a tub of glue. "Think about it and let me know."

I nod and head back to my seat.

"You in trouble?" Tyler asks, sounding worried.

"No," I admit. "She just asked me to do makeup for the winter play."

At this, Tyler grins. "Check you out, getting hired by the school."

I make a face. "Well, I don't think I'm being *hired*; I mean, they're not going to pay me or anything."

He shrugs. "Still kind of cool, though, right?"

"Yeah, I guess."

Tyler pushes the tub of glue over so that it's in between us, along with a stack of magazines. For the last week, we've been combing through old copies of *National Geographic*, cutting out snippets that we can paste together to create something new. I'm working on a sea monster, à la Winston, albeit a little more old-school; Tyler is making a robot out of words. For a few minutes, we work quietly, side by side. I swing my legs back and forth as I work.

Tyler glances over. "Cool boots."

I feel myself blushing. "Thanks. I got them for my birthday."

"Oh man, happy birthday! Why didn't you tell me?"

I shrug. "I don't know."

"That's so cool to have your birthday right around Halloween. Are you having a party or anything? Or are you just going to celebrate at the dance?"

"Oh, I'm not going to the dance."

His eyes widen. "Really? Why not? You got something against awkward middle school functions?"

I laugh. "Something like that."

"So, what are you going to do instead?"

"You mean after all the makeup appointments? I guess I'll just watch some horror movies and pass out candy."

Tyler lets out an exaggerated moan so loud that Mrs. Anderson asks him if he's OK. "I'm cool, Mrs. A. Just jealous."

I look at him. "What are you jealous of?"

"You! You get to have my ideal night. Meanwhile, I'm going to be stuck taking rubbish interviews at the dance."

"Your editor's making you go?"

Tyler narrows his eyebrows. "Co-editor, and yes."

"Do you have to stay the whole time?"

He shrugs. "Not sure yet. We're supposed to figure out the plan tomorrow during lunch."

I nod and continue to work, hoping that he'll keep the conversation going. Normally when I talk to people, I feel a slight pressure in my chest that doesn't seem to go away, no matter how long I've known the person. But with Tyler, I don't feel that weight. Talking to him feels—I don't know. *Easy.*

"This doesn't look much like a robot, does it?" he asks, frowning at his collage.

It doesn't; it looks more like a fork. I reach over and uncap my Sharpie. "Want a little help?" I ask, poised with my marker over his piece.

"I want a lot of help."

I start to sketch out a form over what he already has pasted down. I feel his eyes on me as I work, and it makes my hand shake slightly.

"There," I say, sitting back. "I mean it's not perfect—"

"It's completely perfect. Wow. I can't believe you drew that so fast. It's like a legit robot now! Not some dodgy rectangle."

I feel warm all over. "You can start to fill it in with your collage pieces. Try to keep the darker colors over here for shading." I show him with a few cutouts. "And then the lighter ones over here like this."

A snippet of magazine gets glued to my wrist as I work; I don't notice until Tyler gently peels it off. He holds it up and smiles at me just as the bell rings.

"I guess that's a wrap for today," he says with a sigh.

"Guess so." I hope that my voice doesn't sound as regretful as I feel.

"Later, Marion."

"See you, Tyler."

I hold my breath until he leaves, and only then do I allow myself to smile.

CHAPTER 3

Hours later at home, I can still feel the warmth from Tyler's fingers on my wrist. I'm thankful for the quiet, empty house; it gives me time to collect my thoughts.

Mom sends me a text telling me that she'll be home around four thirty, and that I'm to do my homework right after school. **No Winston,** she writes. **Homework!**

Sighing, I trudge up the stairs to my room, where I hover at the divider and look longingly at my makeup studio. *No, Marion. Be responsible.* I've still got a slew of unfinished and late assignments that were due last week. Sometimes I find it hard to focus on schoolwork, and lately that's showing up in my grades.

I pull the split door closed and fall onto my bed, dropping my backpack on the floor. A poster of the Wolf Man stares at me from across the room, his furry face scrunched up into a semi-silly scowl. I wonder if I can write about were-wolves for my language arts assignment. Probably, right? I'm pretty sure their origins trace back to the 1800s or something. I grab my laptop and start googling.

My search starts off completely focused: find the original werewolf legend; take some notes that I can share in class tomorrow. But after about ten minutes, I become curious about other types of monsters, and my googling starts to shift from werewolves to vampires, from vampires to sea creatures, and the sea creatures obviously make me think of Winston. I soon fall down the rabbit hole of folklore, landing on the legends of the Finfolk, the sea creatures from the Shetland and Orkney Islands. As I click through the images, I realize that these monsters are even more sinister looking than mine. I wonder if the blue dots around Winston's nose are going to be enough. I might need to add some extra shading around the eyes to really bring the menace.

I'm already moving toward my studio before I can stop myself, my books and laptop left behind on my bed. *Five minutes can't hurt*, I tell myself, *then I'll be right back on track before Mom gets home.*

I start by loading the black paint into my airbrush and spray a bit on a test sheet of paper until I figure out the depth of color that I need. Then, I start to work in tiny, careful strokes beneath Winston's hollow eyes—I don't want to overdo it. I just want to give his gaze a more menacing glare, using the darker shade to build a shadow. After just a few moments, the added layer makes it seem like Winston is looking right at me, even though his eyeholes are still empty. Satisfied, I clean out my airbrush and reload the blue that I was using this morning. I add few more dots around the nose for texture, before standing back and appraising my work.

"So close."

I debate adding a bit of gold to the brow line, but I think I used the last of it while pre-painting one of the Halloween dance pieces. Suddenly, I remember Stella. *Let's see what I've got for you.* I begin digging through my stockpile of noses until I find one generic, bent witch's nose, complete with a bulbous wart on the tip. It's not my all-time best work, but it will do in a pinch. I quickly swap out canisters of paint from blue to green in my airbrush and begin spraying and building color, adding shades of brown and gray. It feels as though I've barely gotten started when a throat clears behind me.

I spin around and come face-to-face with my mom.

I drop the witch's nose on the counter.

"Mom. It's not—I just . . ."

She cocks an eyebrow and folds her arms across her chest. "Did you do your homework?"

I don't answer.

"Did you even *start* your homework?"

"Technically, yes," I say, which isn't a total lie.

Mom's not having it, though. "Come on, Marion. You've got to meet me halfway. I mean, I'm all for artistic expression, but if your social studies teacher emails me one more time telling me you're missing your homework . . ." She trails off, shaking her head. "You know the deal. I only let you stay home on Halloween if you're caught up on your assignments."

"I know, I know," I mumble.

"Clean your airbrush and meet me downstairs in five. *With* your homework." She spins around and leaves before I can argue.

I follow orders and clean out my airbrush, placing everything back in its proper place. The witch's nose actually looks pretty good—I was lucky to finish it just as Mom walked in. Hopefully, Stella will be able to glue it on straight by herself. If not, oh well: she'll just be a wonky witch.

I place it on a stand to dry overnight, and then I open my top drawer, which holds my other pre-painted pieces, all ready to go for Friday. One catches my eye: Bea Goodie's sharp cheekbones that Quinn will wear. I think back to lunch earlier today: what was *with* Quinn and her friend Mike? They almost seemed freaked out by the idea of this makeup, almost as if they were afraid of their old neighbors. So, why would she want to dress up like one? *Weird.*

I whack the drawer closed, slamming it harder than I meant; the force rattles the desk and everything on its surface, including Winston. It's like his entire head has suddenly turned, allowing him to stare me down. For a second, the two empty holes seem to be replaced with the most threatening pair of cold, serpent-like eyes. I gasp, nearly tipping over my stool. But when I look back up, Winston's eyes are hollow and empty.

It's just a mask, I tell myself, but I can't help noticing the goose bumps lining my arm as I reach to turn off the hanging light.

"Marion!" Mom calls from downstairs.

"Coming!" I yell back, and with this I fly out of the room without giving my monster a second glance.

Mom is already dicing through a mountain of vegetables by the time I make it to the kitchen.

"Want help?" I ask, eyeing her as she drives a knife down hard over an onion.

"Nope." She points the knife toward the table. "Sit. Homework. Now."

I drop my binder onto the table and slump over my algebra worksheet. I work through formulas as I listen to the thud of Mom's knife on the wooden board: it soon becomes like white noise, and it isn't long before I fall into a rhythm of numbers, letters, and lines, making sense of what seemed nonsensical only moments before.

Once math is done, I move on to science, finishing up a lab report from class. By the time Mom puts the ingredients into a pot to sizzle, I've moved on to language arts, and as the kitchen fills with fragrant, comforting spices, I finish my write-up on Finfolk.

"Good timing," Mom says as I push my binder away. "Chili's ready."

"Aren't we going to wait for Dad? And Margot?"

"Dad said to eat without him—working late. Some kind of engine emergency or something. And Margot's eating at Shivali's house."

Shivali is Margot's best friend. I feel like she eats there more often than she eats here. Mom beckons to me with an empty bowl. "Come on, dig in."

I follow her toward the counter, where we both scoop large helpings of chili into our bowls, topping them with scallions, aged cheddar cheese, cilantro, and sour cream. I sprinkle a few crispy tortilla strips onto mine before carrying it back to the table. Mom joins me, handing me a fork.

"How was school?" she asks.

I take a hot bite, the spices dancing on my tongue. "Fine."

"Anything exciting happen?"

I picture Tyler's finger prying the piece of magazine off my wrist. "No. Same old." I take another bite. "Oh, I guess one thing happened. Mrs. Anderson asked me to be the official makeup artist for the winter play. It's *Little Shop of Horrors.*"

Mom's eyes widen. "Did you say yes?"

"She told me I didn't have to answer her yet. She told me to think about it."

Mom spears a kidney bean with her fork and then points it at me. "This must be what the tarot cards were talking about—the change that was coming!"

"It's not a done deal, Mom."

"Well, it should be. I would totally say yes. I mean, what an opportunity! You should tell her tomorrow that you're interested. You do half of the makeups anyway for the kids who don't want their parents doing theirs. You might as well get the credit."

"But I get paid when I do it on the side. I won't get paid if I'm legit."

Mom narrows her dark eyes, considering this. Finally, she shrugs. "I still think it's a good opportunity. You can make your money in the spring when all of the regular dances start popping up. You'll have your fancy new airbrush in no time."

I scowl. "I'm still not awesome at beauty makeup, though."

"Practice makes perfect."

"Easy for you to say."

"It *is* easy for me to say, because I've had a lot of practice."

We continue to eat side by side, our bowls quickly emptying. When we finish, I help Mom wash the dishes while dancing along to one of her rockabilly records. By the time Dad and Margot come home, Mom and I are sprawled across the couch, sharing a blanket. The TV is on in the background as Mom scrolls through her phone and I doodle beside her.

Margot curls up into the big armchair with a book, and Dad collapses next to us with his own bowl of chili.

"How are my girls?" he asks us. "Good days?"

Margot and I flash him the thumbs-up sign, and Mom rests her head against Dad's shoulder as he eats.

"Got an A on my English test," Margot says, not looking up from her book.

"That's my girl," Mom says with a grin.

I catch Margot's content little smile before she turns the page. My eyes shift back to the TV. The local news has come on. Dad is about to change the channel, but he stops when Rebecca Hayden comes on the screen. She's an old high school friend of Mom's, and Mom still does her makeup every now and again.

"You hear we're getting some wild moon on Friday night?" Dad asks through a spoonful of chili.

"It's Halloween—everything's wild," Mom mutters.

"Nah. This is like something major. Supposed to cause all kinds of flooding. Wait, here's the weather. They'll probably mention it—listen."

We turn back to the screen just as the meteorologist—a tall, clean-shaven man—steps into view. His smile seems too genuine for the TV. Sure enough, though, one of the first things he mentions is the moon.

"Keep an eye in the sky for the Super Blue Blood Moon this Halloween . . ."

Mom snorts. "That's a mouthful."

"Shh," I tell her. "I want to hear this." I grab the remote from Dad and turn up the volume on the TV.

"A *super* moon just means that the moon looks extra bright," the meteorologist explains, "and it's *blue* because it's the second full moon of the month."

"Huh," Mom says. "Learn something new every day."

"I already knew that," Dad tells her.

She pats his knee. "Sure, you did, honey."

Dad pretends to be offended. "I did!" he insists.

"At the end of the total lunar eclipse," the meteorologist continues, "the moon will have a reddish tint. The eclipse might produce a Supermoon Storm, where extra strong winds and unusually high ocean tides can cause extreme flooding onshore. Those along the coastline should stay tuned for updates."

Dad turns to me. "Isn't the school dance being held at Merrick's?"

"The community center?" Mom asks. "I thought it was always held at the school?"

I shake my head. "The student council thought it'd feel more special or whatever if it were held off campus. So, they booked Merrick's." I picture the little community center on the beach, raised on stilts above the crashing waves. The building itself is nothing fancy, but it has a whole wall of windows along the back, so you can see all the way out to Long Island. I imagine the waves rising like the weatherman predicts they will, getting high enough to flood the dance beneath the light of an eerie ruby moon. It would ruin everyone's night—not to mention my makeups, my hours upon hours spent sculpting, molding, painting.

"Well, I guess Winston is the perfect mask for you," Mom says, smirking. "I'm sure a sea monster would love a good flood."

I stiffen on the couch beside her. "I'm not wearing Winston."

She blinks. "Oh, then what are you wearing?"

Dad drops his fork into his empty bowl with a loud clink. "She's not going."

"Don't be ridiculous, of course she's going. Tell him, Marion."

My skin grows so hot that I have to kick the blanket off of my feet. I start snapping the rubber band against my wrist, counting backward from five: *four, three, two, one* . . .

"Why is this such a big deal?" I demand. "I've literally never gone to a school dance before."

"But this is your last Halloween one. The high school only has formal dances."

"So? I probably won't go to those either."

Margot is pretending not to listen, but she hasn't turned a page in her book in ages. I feel Mom and Dad looking at each other, and for some reason this infuriates me more than their goading.

"I'm going upstairs," I mumble. I start to get up, but Dad pulls me gently back onto the couch.

"Honey," he says. "We're not trying to give you a hard time."

"Could've fooled me."

He sighs, holding up his hands. "Consider the subject dropped."

Mom looks at him as if to say, *What's going on?* I assume that as soon as I go upstairs, Dad will fill her in on the conversation we had on the drive to school. I stand up, figuring that I'll save them some time.

"I'm going to check on Winston," I say, heading toward the stairs.

"You sure, honey? You don't want to watch a movie with

us or something? We can throw on An *American Werewolf in London.*"

"I'm sure."

"OK, don't be too long in the workshop. We'll be up later to say good night."

I don't answer as I make the climb up. I hear my parents' low voices follow me as I walk.

"... do you think we should make her go?"

"We can't do that ..."

"But aren't you worried that she doesn't have any friends? I can't remember a kid inviting her over since she was eight. And then—"

"I know," Dad says, cutting her off softly. "I remember."

I run the rest of my way to my room and slam the door loud enough for them to hear. My entire body burns with shame as I barrel into my workshop; not even Winston's now-perfect nose is enough to make me feel better.

I ball my hands into fists as I pace the length of my room, Dr. Magesh's voice in my ear: *"Use your strategies. Be mindful about your feelings. When you start to feel that pressure in your chest or that tingling in your fingers, count backward and focus on an object."* I snap the rubber band in short, quick motions until my skin turns pink. It seems stupid—how is this little rubber band supposed to make me feel better? But it does: time and time again, it does, kind of like my own personal reset button. *Five, four, three ...*

By the time I'm done counting, I can't even hear Mom and Dad's voices anymore. I hate that they worry about me. I hate that they know how lonely I am. Not even the Misfit Toys count as friends—they're just tablemates. And everyone else at school only speaks to me around Halloween because they want some help with their costumes. Usually I don't care that much; the quiet calms me and helps me focus on my work. But sometimes—just sometimes—

There's a soft knock on my bedroom door. I ignore it, digging my nails into my palm.

"It's me," Margot's voice calls. "Can I come in?"

"Fine," I mutter, knowing full well that she's going to come in regardless.

I walk out of my workshop just as the door creaks open. Margot slips into my room. She eyes me for a moment, evaluating her approach. I hate that—I don't want people thinking I'm fragile. Finally, she kicks off her shoes, before climbing into my bed. Sighing, I cross the room, slumping down beside her.

She doesn't speak, and neither do I. She places a hand on my wrist, just over the rubber band. The pressure from her fingers seems to relieve some of the pressure in my head. I know what she's doing: she's checking my pulse to see how fast it's racing.

"Margot, I—"

"Shh," she whispers. "You don't have to talk yet. Let's just count."

Nodding, I pull myself up against the pillow so that we're sitting parallel. Margot leans against the headboard, closes her eyes, and begins counting softly in French. "*Un. Deux. Trois...*"

She keeps going until I eventually start counting with her, our voices low and monotone, sounding like one. By the time she lets go of my wrist, I don't feel the urge to snap the band anymore. She looks at me.

"They don't mean it, you know," she says.

I nod, knowing she's right. "I just don't like them worrying so much about me. It's ..." I trail off, not wanting to admit that it's embarrassing.

Margot arches one of her brows. "Marion, for real. Look around." She gestures toward my studio. "They get you. Give them a break. I mean, would it kill you to go to the dance for an hour? I bet people would be really happy to see you there."

"How do you know that?"

"I know how people are in middle school." She makes a face, remembering her own time at Rocky Hill. "But everyone seems to think you're cool."

At this, I blink. "You really think they like me?"

"I know so." She flashes a devilish grin. "Especially *Tyler*."

My jaw drops before I manage to play it cool. "How do you know about Tyler?"

"I have my ways."

"Whatever." I whack her with a pillow.

She laughs and hits me back, before standing up. "You OK?"

I nod.

She offers a sliver of a smile. "All right, I'm going to go do my homework then." And with this, she disappears just as quietly as she entered.

I stare at the closed door for a few seconds before I sulk back into my workshop. I pick up my airbrush, feeling the cold metal against my skin; it revives me. I manage to find another canister of gold paint in the back of my drawer. Without a second thought, I load it and run a few test sprays against my wrist, turning my skin into something ornate and almost ethereal. Perfect. Raising the gun to Winston, I shoot, working my hand back and forth, lightly, so lightly, just enough to give a halo effect around the sides. By the time I step back, Winston is positively glowing. I lean forward and inspect him closer—and as I do so, the edges of his mouth twist up into a menacing smile.

"Ahh!"

I jump back just as my phone vibrates on the table beside me. I leave it there buzzing as I shoot another cautious look at Winston. Everything seems to be in order: his mouth is an open gash of rubber. No smile. No smirk. No movement. Nothing out of the ordinary.

Get a grip, Marion.

My phone vibrates again, bouncing along the counter. I squint at the screen, before picking it up. Unknown Number. Weird. I open the text.

Hey, the message reads, **it's Tyler.**

I nearly drop my phone. I stare at the screen for what feels like forever before another message appears. **I know, sorry. This makes me look like a creepy stalker doesn't it? I got your number from Eitan.**

Eitan? I make a mental note to buy him a cookie tomorrow at lunch.

You're not creepy, I type back, hitting SEND before I can chicken out or say something stupid. **What's up?**

My heart beats faster as I wait for his response. **Check this out.** He attaches a photograph of his art collage, the robot I helped him with—only now it's filled in more around the top with little magazine cutouts. It's not finished, but it actually looks like a machine as opposed to a fork.

Looks great, I write, before immediately smacking my palm against my forehead. Was that dumb? Should I have said something funny? Tyler likes funny.

Tyler sends back a selfie of him grinning with the robot. His smile is everything.

Twins, I write.

Except I'm way better looking. Obviously.

I don't know how to respond to that, so I just send a robot emoji and hope for the best.

See you tomorrow, Marion.

Night, Tyler.

I switch off the overhead light and close up shop, before collapsing onto my bed. I fall asleep with a smile.

The smile doesn't last long, though.

In my dream, I'm on the beach, standing on the sand at the edge of town. I can see the community center in the distance, balanced precariously on stilts as the waves crash against it. My classmates are pressed against the big picture windows, their faces painted in the most horrified expressions. They call to me, but my Docs are stuck, as if the sand has been replaced with concrete. I feel my heart beating faster as the storm comes, pounding me with rain all of a sudden. Lightning flashes dangerously close to my fogged-up glasses. I watch the waves grow higher, and the entire seascape seems to turn black and white and gray, losing all shades of color and warmth.

And that's when I see it. *Him.* I see Winston. Slinking toward me with a full fish-monster body, his gills flapping with each movement, scales reflecting the lightning that cuts across the sky. My throat is too dry to scream, as if it's been filled with sand. The waves crash closer to us, like Winston is somehow controlling their proximity, commanding them to follow each of his footprints. My classmates beat against the glass in warning. But I can't move, not even when Winston is upon me, his seaweed scent filling my nose as the waves wash over me, pushing me into the clutches of a monster. My monster.

I wake up drenched in sweat, barely able to catch my breath. My eyes flash over to my workshop, and even though my entire body is aching with fear, I force myself out of bed, stumbling toward the divider. *I just need to check . . .*

Slowly, I open the door and inch forward, little by little. I don't know what I'm expecting to see when I flip on the overhead light, but I can't help but gasp as I tug the string, squeezing my eyes shut.

Four . . . three . . . two . . . I take a breath and peek through my fingertips. Winston's still there, just where I left him on the foam head. His face is hollow and lifeless, without moving gills or pointy teeth.

It's just a mask, I tell myself. *Just a mask.*

And with a fast swipe, I tug on the string once more, leaving us both in the dark.

CHAPTER 4

It takes me forever to fall asleep again, but once I finally do, I don't dream. When I wake up the next morning, the nightmare feels like a fuzzy, washed-out memory.

"Morning, honey," Mom says, greeting me in the kitchen. She holds out a steaming cup of my favorite pumpkin spice coffee. "Got you this and a muffin from Dunkin'. It's still warm." She dangles a brown bag in front of my nose.

"Thanks." The events of last night come back to me. I know what this is: an *I'm sorry for saying that you don't have any friends* muffin. I should tell her that I'm not hungry. I should drop the muffin into the garbage can with a dramatic thud. But in truth, it smells too good and I'm too hungry.

"Where's my muffin?" Dad asks, pouting as he comes into the kitchen.

Mom hands him a cup of coffee instead. "Best I can do,"

she tells him. "They only had two pumpkin muffins. And the other one is for Margot."

Dad flops down beside me and steals a big bite of mine before I can swat his hand away. "Just testing it," he tells me. "Don't worry, it's good."

"Dad!" I pull the bag closer to me and begin to devour its deliciousness. I can't even pretend to be mad anymore.

On cue, Mom sidles over to me, her face drooping with uncertainty and guilt. "About last night . . ." she starts.

I wave her off. "I'm fine, Mom. It's cool."

"But honey, I—"

"I added gold to Winston," I blurt out, desperate to change the subject. The only thing worse than having parents who think you don't have any friends is having parents who want to constantly talk about how you don't have any friends. "It looks really good. You should go see it before you leave." I make a pointed glance toward the cobweb-covered stairs.

Mom's eyes hover on mine for a moment before she slowly nods. "OK, sure. I'll be back in a minute." I watch her spin around in her platforms, her skirt swirling as she makes her way upstairs. For a moment, she reminds me of a Disney princess, like a punk rock Snow White, and the thought makes me remember being a kid and sitting beside her at her vanity, watching her apply her makeup in the morning and wishing that one day I would grow up to be as pretty as her.

"Eat up, Mar, we've got to leave in five," Dad tells me, breaking the trance in the room. I shove the rest of my breakfast into my mouth and excuse myself to brush my teeth upstairs.

On my way to the bathroom, I find Mom coming out of my room, her eyes bright.

"It's beautiful," she gushes, squeezing my arms. "You've got something special in there, Marion. I'm so incredibly proud of you." And before I can answer, she pulls me in for a tight, tight hug, where I lose myself in her soft black hair and the smell of orange blossoms.

"I love you," she whispers into the top of my head. I squeeze back.

"Let's go!" Dad calls from the kitchen.

At the sound of his voice, Mom releases me, checking her watch. "I have to jet, too. I've got an early booking." She runs a hand gently across my cheek. "Have a great day, honey."

"You too, Mom."

With one last smile, she turns to go downstairs. I bolt into the bathroom to brush my teeth, and by the time I make my way back to the kitchen, Mom is gone. Margot is perched on the edge of one of the chairs, scarfing what's left of her muffin as she waits for Shivali to pick her up. She nods to me, and I nod back. Dad is leaning impatiently against the counter, jangling his keys.

"Ready," I tell him. "Bye, Margot."

"Bye, sweetie," Dad tells her.

"Later," she tells us.

Dad hands me my backpack and my Count Chocula lunch box, and together we step outside into the warm October sun.

Thankfully, Dad doesn't say anything today about the dance; instead, he drives with his music cranked up, singing along with the windows cracked. I give him a fist bump as we park in front of the school—our new thing, apparently.

"See you later, sweetheart."

"Bye, Dad."

I let the door slam behind me as I move quickly toward the building, my mind now completely focused on Tyler: Will he be waiting by my locker again today? Will he mention last night? What if I don't see him before art class? Then I will have to wait all morning just to talk to him . . .

The hallway seems even more crowded and excited than it usually is the day before Halloween. If this were a movie, a killer song would cut through the noise, and everyone would stomp in slow motion to their homerooms. But since it's not a movie, everyone is pushing and running—it's borderline chaos.

The dance posters still dangle above our heads, and as I approach my locker, I notice that there's still a flyer taped to it. Peeling it off, I gently fold it and place it into my bag.

You know, just for a souvenir. I'm most definitely not going to the dance.

I do a quick survey of the hallway, my stomach flipping as I look for Tyler, but he's nowhere to be seen. With a sigh, I grab my notebooks and make my way to homeroom.

Everyone is hyper in every class, and it's a struggle for the teachers to keep us focused. I'm sure it will be worse tomorrow, which makes me extra thankful that I get to stay home.

Dad's words flutter through my mind: *"Don't you want to at least see all of your monsters out there in the wild?"* I shake this thought away, and instead start doodling in my composition notebook while Mr. Dupois calls people up to share their favorite folktale. I grip my pencil tighter in my hand, hoping that the kids ahead of me will talk for so long that we won't have time for everyone to present. No. Such. Luck.

"Marion," he says, beckoning me up with a smile. "Let's hear about your legend."

I snap my pencil in two at the sound of my name. Maybe if I sit really, really still, he won't see me? *It's worth a try.*

Mr. Dupois clears his throat. "Marion?"

I feel someone nudge my shoulder from behind. It's Mike Warren. "Hey, Monster Makeup Girl. You're on."

Thank you, Captain Obvious. But I get up, forcing my legs to move with one step in front of the other until I'm standing in front of the entire class, with my hands stuffed inside the pockets of my black skinny jeans. I can't meet anyone's eye.

Mr. Dupois claps his hands together with a little too much enthusiasm. "And what legend did you research last night, Marion?"

"Finfolk," I say quietly—perhaps a bit too quietly, since Mr. Dupois cups his hand against his ear.

"Speak up, dear."

Dear. Is that supposed to make me feel more at ease? Because if anything, it is making me feel even more nauseous.

"She said *Fin-folk*, Mr. Dupois," Mike Warren calls loudly from his seat. "You know, like mer-maids. Half people, half fish." He speaks slowly, as if explaining something to a toddler.

Mr. Dupois frowns at him. "Thank you, Mike, but I think Marion is capable of explaining her own research." He nods to me. "Please continue."

Once again, my stomach tightens and I stare at my Docs, willing the green shimmer to calm me. I think of Winston and take a long, deep breath. *Just get it over with, Marion.*

Mr. Dupois must notice my nerves. "Why don't you just grab your homework paper? It's OK, you can take it up there with you. You didn't have to have this memorized."

Heat rushes through me as I go to my desk and fumble through my notebook, feeling everyone's stares as I find the paper. Then, with heavy steps, I return to the front of the room. *All I have to do is read the words. Easy.* I force my eyes onto the page. "Finfolk were thought to be shape-shifters of the sea," I say, my voice rough around the edges. "But they weren't mermaids," I add, making quick eye contact with Mike, who is smiling at me and nodding along in his smug way, as if he knew the whole time that mermaids and Finfolk were different.

"How are they different?" Mr. Dupois asks, as though he's actually interested.

I take another deep breath, shifting the paper to one hand so that I can pinch the rubber band between my fingers. "Mermaids weren't shape-shifters like the Finfolk. And mermaids weren't as malicious. Finfolk were said to go ashore and abduct humans—"

"Yeah," Mike interrupts. "And take them back into the sea."

Mr. Dupois sighs. "Mike . . ."

Before Mike can respond, someone asks a question from the back of the room. "Did the humans die in the sea?"

"Usually," Mike tells them. "But sometimes they'd keep their favorites alive."

"Mike," Mr. Dupois says with a firm voice. "Let Marion speak."

I open my mouth, but nothing comes out. The words on the page become blurry, and all I can see are the many faces staring expectantly at me, waiting for an answer. I *know* the answer: the Finfolk would fill their lungs with magic air to let them breathe underwater. Then the humans would be forced to stay in the sea forever. No freedom. No choice. No escape.

But I don't say any of this. Instead, I shift my weight, snapping the rubber band.

Mr. Dupois gives me a small nod. "Thank you, Marion. You can sit down." Then he turns to Mike. "Mr. Warren, am I correct in assuming that you also researched the Finfolk?"

Mike is already standing up, gathering his notes. "Is it my turn?" He saunters up to the front of the room, where I'm still standing frozen.

"You can sit down now," he whispers.

I hear a giggle from the corner, and the horrid sound magically unfreezes my feet. I escape to my desk, counting in my head to slow down the racing of my heart. *Three, two, one* . . .

Meanwhile, Mr. Dupois carries on as though nothing happened. "How did the Finfolk abduct people?" he asks Mike, who's standing up there with all the confidence in the world. For a moment, I hate him for it.

"They'd trick the humans," Mike explains. "Sometimes they would take the form of a fisherman on a rowboat, or a really hot girl, or even a patch of seaweed—which is weird, now that I think about it."

Mr. Dupois nods. "Definitely weird. And what are the origins of this legend?"

"Orkney and Shetland," Mike says without missing a beat. "Locals used these legends to explain the disappearance of fishermen or women lost at sea." He shrugs. "I don't know—seems kind of wild to me. Wouldn't it have just made more sense to say that someone was shipwrecked or they drowned?"

"Of course," Mr. Dupois says, "but the whole point of these legends is that they provided a distraction to the locals. In most cases, the truth was too terrible for them to face. Inventing monsters was almost easier." He motions for Mike to sit down.

"Good job, partner," Mike says to me as he passes.

I can't tell if he's serious, so I just put my head down for the rest of class.

At lunch, Shannon and Tanya start squealing as soon as I reach the table.

"We heard about Mrs. Anderson's offer," Shannon cries, tugging dramatically on my sleeve. "You have to do it! Tanya and I are in the play."

"Yeah, you can do our makeup."

I sit down next to Carter and unlatch my lunch box. "I'm thinking about it."

Janae approaches and shoos them to their seats. "I told you to give her space," she scolds her friends, plopping down beside me.

"How do you even know about it?" I ask, pulling out my sandwich.

Shannon bats her eyes. "I have my sources."

"Your sources should have told you that it's not definite," I tell her. "I haven't said *yes*, yet."

"But what's there to think about?" Shannon moans, tearing open her bag of chips. She crunches a handful loudly, the crumbs spilling out of her mouth. "It's *Little Shop of Horrors*! And *us*!" She waves between herself and Tanya. "What's not to like?"

Before I can answer, Eitan slides in with his overflowing plate of french fries. "So what's the plan for our game tomorrow?" he asks, steering the conversation into Dungeons & Dragons land and inadvertently pushing me to the side.

The girls and Carter attack his fries, and together they laugh and make plans for their next adventure. I sit on the edge and pick at my sandwich, feeling even more like a misfit at the table of Misfit Toys.

Mom's words pop into my head: "*Aren't you worried that she doesn't have any friends?*" I shift uncomfortably in my seat, pushing my sandwich away.

"You not going to eat that?" Shannon asks, eyeing it up.

"It's yours if you want," I tell her. "I'm not really hungry."

The bell takes forever to ring, and at its sound, my feet glide on autopilot, pulling me toward art class. My heart rate quickens with each step. By the time I turn the corner into the room, Tyler is already perched on his stool, his face hidden by a mop of curls as he bends over his collage.

"Hey," I say, taking a seat beside him.

He looks up and grins at me, his smile so full and bright that it causes my stomach to drop.

"Marion! Check it out." He holds up his picture, which is significantly more filled out than it was last night.

I give it an appraising eye, trying my best to look professional and artsy, and not at all like I'm about to hyperventilate under his stare.

"It looks better," I tell him.

"*Better*? Just better? Come on, Marion, you can at least say it looks *good*. I spent an hour cutting out little scraps of paper last night. My mom yelled at me because I ruined her copy of *Popular Science*."

I laugh and pull out my own collage. "It looks good, Tyler."

He squints at the paper. "Promise?"

"Promise."

"Cool." He flips open a new magazine and hands me one. "Let's get cutting."

We snip away for a few minutes silently. I can feel him

looking at me from the corner of his eye, but I don't dare meet his gaze until he speaks again.

"So . . ."

I gulp. "So?"

"You still boycotting the dance tomorrow night?"

"I'm not *boycotting* the dance. I'd just rather stay home and watch movies."

Tyler raises his eyebrows. "So, you haven't gotten roped into playing Dungeons & Dragons, the Halloween Edition?"

"Nope." I look at him. "You?"

He laughs. "Nah. Eitan got me to try it once, but I got annoyed when I couldn't be the evil monster, so I quit."

"Why did you want to be evil? You're so nice." The words escape my lips before I can pull them back, and instantly I feel my face grow hot.

Tyler grins. "You think I'm nice?"

I bow my head and start gluing like mad.

"How's it going over here?" Mrs. Anderson asks, saving me from further embarrassment. "Wow, Tyler. I like the work you put in last night. Have you seen this, Marion?"

"Yeah, she's the one who helped save it," Tyler says, nudging my arm.

"Well, I think you owe her your life," Mrs. Anderson says with a wink. "Or at least a milkshake." She shuffles past us toward the next table.

Tyler leans over to peer at my creature. "You are

ridiculously good at this stuff." His eyes light up. "Hey, can I interview you for the paper? Eitan said you might be into it. I could add you to the Halloween spread—it'd be perfect."

My heart flutters as I meet his eyes. "I *guess*?"

He laughs. "Don't sound too excited."

"I'm sorry," I say, feeling myself blush. "I've just never been interviewed before."

"It's easy—you don't have to be nervous," he tells me. "We can do a practice question right now, if you want."

I shrug. "OK."

He twists his lips and looks at the ceiling, thinking of something to ask me. "OK, OK, I got one." He clears his throat. "What makeup are you most proud of?"

"That's easy: Winston."

"Who's Winston?"

I smile and straighten my glasses. "He's this sea creature I'm working on. My first full mask. Everything else I've made have been small, separate prosthetic pieces, but Winston is the biggest creature I've ever molded."

Tyler doesn't seem to notice that he's dropped his pencil. "Do you name all of your monsters?"

"Some of them."

"Can I see it?"

"What? Winston?"

Tyler nods, his eyes widening as if he's just had the most amazing idea. "I found out at lunch that I only have to go to the dance for an hour. So, I can maybe stop by before to take some photos and we can finish the interview. Then after the dance, maybe I can come back and crash your movie marathon?"

"Umm . . . I . . ." My fingers start tingling.

His face drops. "I mean, only if you don't already have plans. But if you'd rather go play the game with Janae and them, I get it."

"No, I—"

"Or would you rather be alone? Because I definitely understand—"

It takes me placing my hand on his elbow for him to stop talking. I feel a buzz of electricity from the soft corner of his sleeve, and the jolt makes me feel more alive than I've ever felt before. "You can come," I tell him, finding my voice and my courage in his smile. "I mean, if you want to . . ."

"I want to," he says quickly, running a hand through his wild hair. He almost looks bashful. "What are we watching?"

"I have two on deck," I say, listing them: "Definitely *Pumpkinhead* and *The Thing.*"

"We need a third," Tyler says.

"Three? But that would take, like, six hours to watch."

"Two movies isn't a 'marathon,' though. *Three* is a marathon. Does it have to be from the eighties?"

I nod. "Always. They have the best makeup and special effects."

He shrugs. "OK. Then I vote for *Gremlins*."

I squint at him. "That's a Christmas movie."

"No, it's not!"

"It most definitely is. And it isn't even scary."

"That's a matter of opinion—I was scared to death of that movie when I was little. Besides, I like Gizmo. *Gremlins* stays."

But there isn't any makeup in Gremlins, I almost say. Whine—I almost whine, and while I may not be an expert on all things social, I'm pretty confident that whining is not a way to make someone like you. And I really, *really* want Tyler to like me.

"OK," I tell him. "*Pumpkinhead, The Thing,* and *Gremlins.*"

Tyler claps me on the shoulder like a football coach. "Way to take one for the team, Jones!"

It is in this moment that I realize that I'm still touching his elbow.

"Less talking, more gluing!" Mrs. Anderson says from behind us. Her cheerful voice slices through the air, and I immediately pull my hand back.

Tyler smiles at me and hands me a paintbrush dipped in glue.

CHAPTER 5

I wake up with the sun the next day, its rays streaming through my blinds like gold ribbons. Halloween is the one day I don't mind getting up. Maybe it's because it's the only day that I get permission to skip school.

Any minute now, Mom will be calling the main office and explaining to the secretary that I'll be missing school for "personal reasons." I can almost hear Mrs. Mateo sighing into the receiver—she knows I miss every year, and she knows it's not for illness.

Mom will assure her I'll be back on Monday, and then with a heavy sigh, Mrs. Mateo will check me off on the absentee list, before telling Mom that she hopes I feel better, her voice coated in a thick layer of sarcasm.

"That broad is old-school," Mom said last year after hanging up with Mrs. Mateo. *"I like her."*

For some reason, remembering this makes me smile. Maybe it's the routine of it all: Mom and I have Halloween down like a well-oiled, spooky machine. Ever since I was little, we'd wake up, call out from work and school, and gorge on pumpkin spice pancakes, before making a double batch of fake blood. We'd light all the candles throughout the house, and Mom would blast her Halloween playlists—a mix of psychobilly horror-blues, with just a drop of "Monster Mash" and "Thriller" for good measure. Then we'd assemble my makeup pieces and the goody bags: take-home Ziploc bags containing makeup remover and instructions. Eventually, Margot would come home from school—she has always refused to skip like me—and Dad would come home early from work, and the four of us would carve jack-o'-lanterns until my first client showed up.

It's a day I look forward to year after year, and now I spring out of bed and fumble for my glasses, ready to get started.

"Morning, Sunshine," Mom says, greeting me in the kitchen. "Just spoke to Mrs. Mateo. She's as cheerful as ever." She hands me a cup of pumpkin spice coffee and a plate of pancakes with little bat-shaped sprinkles on top. "Happy Halloween."

I grin. "Happy Halloween."

Together, we bring our plates to the kitchen table, where Mom fans out her full skirt as she takes a seat: the vintage pattern has jack-o'-lanterns printed all over it, and she's paired it with a fitted black-and-white-striped top. As usual, she wears her signature red lipstick, and her dark hair spills over her shoulders in pinup-style waves.

"Eat up," she tells me.

I take a bite, and the pancakes are sugar and spice and everything nice. It doesn't take me long to devour the whole plate, and by the time I finish my coffee, my body is buzzing, ready to begin our tasks.

"Blood time?" I ask, dropping our empty dishes into the sink.

"You know it," Mom says, joining me at the counter.

She leans over and switches on some music, before handing me a pair of bright purple rubber gloves and an apron. Together, we bop our heads along to the heavy and slow rhythm of the upright bass, singing along once the lyrics kick in.

"Do you want the thin or the clotted?" I ask, pulling out two blenders from the cabinet and placing them down on the counter with a thud.

"Oh, the options," Mom says, pretending to think too hard about the choices. "Thin," she finally says, pulling one of the blenders toward her.

I start gathering supplies: dark and light corn syrups, flour, powdered sugar, cocoa, a pitcher of water, and dye. Last year, Mom and I started using water-based paints instead of food coloring so that it doesn't stain everything. The kitchen used to look like a crime scene for days, and my clients' skin would show the remnants of the fake blood for an entire week.

"How much are we making? The regular amounts?"

I nod and pull out two of our largest Tupperwares. "I think if we fill these, it should be enough."

"OK, boss. Let's go."

Since Mom's mixing the thinner blood, I push over the light corn syrup, the powdered sugar, the cocoa, water, and the red paint. I, meanwhile, begin to measure out the ingredients for the thicker, more clotted blood: dark corn syrup, flour, water, red paint, along with extra drops of green and blue so that I can get that richer, more jewel-like color.

"I thought we'd order *fra diavolo* pizza tonight from Cucina Della Nonna," Mom says, pouring the powdered sugar into the blender with the water. She nudges me in the ribs. "Get it? Because *diavolo* means 'devil'?"

I snort. "Yeah, thanks, Mom. I got it." Carefully, I combine the dark corn syrup with the water, mixing it with a spoon before adding the paint, along with a few teaspoons of flour for a clot-like, goopy thickness. This consistency is perfect for making realistic wounds, whereas the thinner blood that Mom makes is better for splattered clothes.

"I got a few extra bags of your favorite candies," she continues, "so we can eat our weight in mallow pumpkins and

Sour Patch in between scaring the trick-or-treaters. And Dad already downloaded the entire Stephen King collection, so all systems are go."

I take a sharp inhale and turn on the blender, holding my palm against the lid. "I actually have plans to watch movies with a friend."

Mom cups her ear. "What?"

"I have plans."

"You *want* plans?"

"No," I shout over the blender. "I *have* plans!"

Mom reaches over and shuts off the machine. "Seriously? With who?"

I shrug and try my best to act casual, like it's no big deal that I'm going to do an eighties movie marathon with Tyler Dash. "Just some kid from school."

Mom nudges me with her hip. "Care to elaborate?"

"Not really."

"Marion!"

I sigh. "OK, OK. His name's Tyler."

"Tyler, huh?"

"Mom, it's really not a big deal." *Even though it is, in fact, a very big deal.* "Can you not make a thing out of it? Please?"

Mom stares at me for a long moment. Neither of us moves. Finally, I see the flicker of a smile. "Of course, honey." And as if nothing has happened, she turns back to her blender, adding a teaspoon of cocoa powder to the mixture.

I breathe a sigh of relief and watch her work, for the first time noticing a tray of skeleton cookies cooling on a tray beside her; she must have made them this morning before I woke up. Mom's cookies are legendary. Grandma Goldie owned a bake shop back in Los Angeles that Mom was going to inherit before she settled here in Connecticut. When Mom's not doing makeup, she's baking. And she's *good*— like, really good. I can practically taste the skeletons already.

My mind drifts to Tyler. I wonder if he'd like one of Mom's cookies, or if he even likes cookies, or what his favorite kind of candy is. I've seen him sneak an Airhead once or twice in art class; the first week of school, he offered me one and our hands touched and I never could bring myself to eat it, even though it was watermelon flavored.

"Earth to Marion," Mom says, her wide eyes focused on me, obviously waiting for an answer to a question that I didn't even hear her ask.

I blink the room back into focus. "Sorry, what?"

She smiles at me, an exaggerated, knowing smile. Her index finger draws a heart in the air. "You're thinking about him, aren't you?" Her voice is light and playful. She pokes me on the end of my nose, leaving a bloody fingerprint: I bet I look like Rudolph the Red-Nosed Reindeer now. I grab a wet paper towel and wipe it off before it dries.

"No," I lie, feeling my face turn as red as the paint.

Mom arches one of her eyebrows. "Liar, liar, pants on fire."

I shake my head at her and switch the blender back on. "You're so immature," I grumble over the roar.

Mom just laughs.

"Since you're already bloody, let me try out a wound." I tell her. "I've been playing around with eyelash glue and eyeshadow instead of latex and paint."

"Allergy?"

I nod. "One client. I told her I could do something small and latex-free."

"Consider me at your service." Mom dives into an exaggerated bow like a butler.

"Cool. But I need your makeup kit."

Mom's eyes widen. "*My* makeup kit? You want to use the good stuff for a gash?"

"Well, it's either that or toothpaste, and I don't know how long the toothpaste will hold up at a dance."

"Fine. You know where it is. But use your own brushes, not my nice ones."

"Got it."

I scurry off to the vintage vanity in her room, and I gather what I need before grabbing my own makeup brush bag on the way back down.

Mom is already seated at the kitchen table, waiting. I sit across from her and pull her arms toward me, studying them like a doctor examining her patient. Her skin is so colorful: I need to find a light base somewhere among all of these tattoos. I decide upon a white mountain laurel that's intertwined with an orange-red poppy: the state flowers to represent Connecticut and California. The mountain laurel is large enough for me to create a narrow wound, so I unpack my supplies and get to work.

First, I use black eyeliner to sketch out where the wound will be. I then outline it with a heavy coat of eyelash glue and top it with tightly rolled strips of toilet paper, twisted so that they resemble the edges of a fake gash. Once they're applied, I take out Mom's foundation, blending with an angled brush, and layering it with a pale-white eyeshadow the same shade as her tattoo.

"It tickles," Mom says with a smile.

"Stay still," I tell her.

I dive back into one of her eyeshadow palettes to dip my brush into one of the pinks, and I apply it to the edges of the wound. Next, I coat the middle of the wound with black liquid liner, before going back over the whole thing with red lipstick applied with a thin, narrow brush, and topping it off with a drop of fake blood. One last sweep of pink to blend it all together, and Mom's arm is looking in desperate need of urgent care.

"Done," I say, sitting back in my chair to appraise my work.

"Ooh la la!" she cries, holding her arm out in front of her. "It looks gruesome. I love it! Here, take a picture of me."

She slides her phone across the table to me and then stands up and poses dramatically, pretending to scream while holding her wounded arm across her forehead like a stereotypical damsel in distress.

"Now you, too," she says, pulling me in close, holding the camera out for a selfie of the two of us. "This is going on all of my accounts," she says with a smile. I don't have any social media of my own yet, but I think it might be cool to start one for my makeup. Mom mainly posts pictures of makeup and baked goods, as well as her vintage clothes—but she has thousands of followers. Sometimes it's hard knowing that she's more popular than me, both in real life and online.

"You OK, sweetie?"

I nod and snap the band against my wrist. "Yeah, I'm fine."

Mom taps her chin, a thoughtful look on her face. "What do you say we capture Winston's first Halloween, too?"

"He's not ready."

"Don't be silly. Of course he's ready. I poked my head in your room this morning—he looks gorgeous. Definitely camera ready."

I throw my eyes to the clock on the microwave. "OK, but we don't have the time for one of your epic photo sessions," I warn her. "One picture, then back to work. Promise?"

She waves two fingers in a salute. "Scout's honor."

"You were never a Girl Scout."

She shrugs one shoulder. "No matter. Come on, stop dillydallying. We're on a schedule, remember?"

I wipe my hands on a paper towel before following Mom upstairs.

"Better clean that bedroom before your clients show up," she says along the way. Her eyes glimmer. "Especially if *Tyler* is coming over."

I freeze, mid-step: Will Tyler Dash actually see my room? Like, my *room* room? The very place where I sleep, and think, and dream—sometimes of him?

I shake my head. *Calm down, Marion,* I try and tell myself. Tyler or not, my room could definitely do with a once-over. Everyone will be marching through here to get to my workshop, and I want them to see a more professional, well-kept space. I want them to know that I'm serious about what I do.

"Dad and Margot are coming home early, right?" I ask.

Mom nods. "They're supposed to be here by two."

"I think I'll have ten or fifteen minutes in between the pumpkin carving and my first client," I say. "Should be enough time to clean up."

I push through to the workshop. Winston is the first thing I see, and as the overhead light switches on and the colors shimmer across his metallic gills, he seems to come alive. I catch my breath.

"He *is* done, isn't he?" I say, more to myself than to my mom.

She nudges me in the arm. "Told you so. Now hurry up, put him on."

She stands back with her phone poised to take a picture. When Dad redid my room, he left one of the side walls white at my request: a kind of built-in backdrop to photograph my finished makeups.

Slowly, I walk over to Winston and lift him off the foam head, feeling the scaly texture of his skin between my fingertips. He was made for me: the mold was cast with my own face, so that even if anyone else tries him on, he won't fit as perfectly as he does on me. Pulling him on now, I breathe in the familiar scents of rubber and paint, and after a moment of darkness, I stare through two unfamiliar peepholes. I blink, and Mom waves me over.

"Come on," she tells me.

I walk over and stand in front of the stark white wall, my body still as Mom snaps a few shots.

"It's amazing, Mar," she tells me. "I think I got it. I mean, they all look good. Here, see?" She holds out her phone for me, and I peel off the mask to check out the photo.

"Wow," I gasp, taking it all in. The latex is perfectly fitted to my face. The edges are smooth, the seams invisible underneath the iridescent paint, the gills fanning out at just the right angles. I zoom in on my eyes, staring out from a monster, which are so sinister and deep that it gives me chills.

"Wow is right, honey. See? I told you makeup is magic."

"It's an illusion, Mom. Not magic."

"Nonsense. I've had loads of magical things happen in the studio when I was younger."

"Like what?"

"Changes in weather. Wishes granted. Those kinds of things."

"Coincidences."

"Don't be such a naysayer all the time." She makes a face before hitting a button on her phone, and I hear a text alert from the corner of my room. "Just sent the picture to you. Now come on—we've got some goody bags to assemble, don't we?"

I nod, before placing Winston back on the stand.

"I'll just run down and find the Ziplocs," Mom says, disappearing through the door.

As soon as she's gone, I grab my phone from the top of my dresser and open to the image she just sent. Up pops my face, only it isn't me: it's a monster. The gills and scales curve in all of the right places, flowing in the same motion as tendrils of seaweed. It's beautiful. My very first mask.

A text message comes through, buzzing in my hands. It's Tyler!

Hey, he writes, followed by an animated photo of

Gizmo doing a little happy dance. **Getting psyched for Gremlins tonight!**

I laugh out loud. Do I send him a picture, too? Something funny? Maybe one of the bad gremlins from the movie? I chew on my bottom lip, my thumbs tapping against the screen. **Can't wait,** I type back, attaching the picture of me wearing my Winston mask. As soon as I hit SEND, I immediately want to take it back.

Thankfully, it takes less than a minute for Tyler to respond: **Brilliant! Is that your newest creation?**

Yup, I reply.

So cool. Can I try it on later? he asks.

My hands tingle as I type **Sure.**

He sends back the thumbs-up sign. I send a smiley face.

See you soon, he says.

OK!!! I write back, instantly regretting the extra exclamation points at the end.

"Too late now," I mumble, hoping that Tyler doesn't think I'm *too* excited, or too eager, or too whatever.

I exhale right as Mom enters the room. She eyes my phone.

"Is that your father?" she asks. "He's not going to be late tonight, is he?"

"No," I answer simply. I drop my phone onto the table and reach out to take the plastic bags from her.

"I thought we'd put some candy in the goody bags, too,"

Mom says, holding up packs of Milky Way and Skittles. "'Cause you know, trick or treat." She grins and tosses a mini chocolate bar to me.

"Thanks." I unwrap the Milky Way and crush it between my teeth, savoring the salty-sweet flavor.

Mom downs a pack of Skittles before switching on her phone and pumping her Halloween playlist throughout the room. Together, we form an assembly line, organizing Q-tips, little bottles of makeup remover, Wet Ones, and typed instructions. One by one, we sing along to the music as we tuck one or two of everything in each Ziploc. By the time Dad's truck rumbles in the driveway, we're done packing all twenty-one bags. Mom high-fives me.

"That seemed like a record," she says. "I think we've earned a cookie. What do you say?"

"Obviously," I tell her. "I've been eyeing those all morning."

She smiles and puts her arm around me, leading me out of the room and down the stairs. When we reach the kitchen, we catch Dad red-handed with a skeleton cookie wedged in his mouth. His eyes widen when he sees us.

"Thrr imun wha ew fink," he mumbles.

"I'm sure it's exactly what I think." Mom arches a brow and pretends to scowl at him. "Unhand those cookies, sir." She holds out her hands to take back the tray; Dad grabs one more cookie before relinquishing the rest.

"They're good," he says, grinning like a kid.

I smile back and take my own, and Dad's right: they are quite possibly Mom's best-ever batch.

"You girls ready to carve?" Dad asks.

"Not without me," Margot says, suddenly standing in the kitchen doorway.

"Wouldn't dream of it," Dad tells her with a smile.

Margot drops her book bag onto the counter and smiles back.

Dad motions to the kitchen table. "Check it out—I already brought in the pumpkins from outside."

"You got the Dremels, too?" I ask, hopping into the seat in front of the largest pumpkin.

"Do you doubt me, daughter?" He gestures over to the counter, where four handheld carving tools sit in a line.

"Are they charged?" Mom asks.

"Of course they are. What do you take me for?" Dad hands one to each of us, before finishing his cookie and joining us at the table.

Usually, I have my pumpkin design mapped out weeks in advance. Today, though, I'm winging it.

"What are you thinking, Marion?" Dad asks. "Zombie? Killer fly?"

I tap a pencil against the side of my pumpkin, taking in the long, oval shape of it, big enough to fit a howling wolf and a moon. "Werewolf," I tell him.

Dad nods. "Inspired by the Super Blue Blood Moon tonight?"

"I guess," I say, picking up a pencil and sketching out my design against the pumpkin's skin. I try to capture the werewolf in mid-change, when the hair is just starting to sprout and the fangs are beginning to form. He looks in pain, with his eyes closed and his (mostly) human head stretched up toward the moon. Once I'm finished drawing, I take a butcher knife and saw off the top of the pumpkin, scooping out the gooey guts and seeds from the inside, inhaling the earthy scent as I go.

Mom flicks on the kitchen TV to the classic movie channel, which to my delight is playing reruns of old monster movies.

"Oh, color me inspired," Mom says, watching *The Bride of Frankenstein* take the screen, her black hair sticking straight up with the white lightning bolt zigzagging down the middle. "Look how chic she is! I would totally wear her white dress to go out."

Dad squints at the screen. "I think you *have* worn that out before."

Mom gently whacks him in the arm. "Forget the witch that I was going to do—I'm going to carve her." She nods to the screen and begins running her pencil over the face of the pumpkin, sketching out the profile of the bride.

"What are you doing, Margot?" Dad asks.

"Quote," Margot mumbles.

"You don't want to try carving a monster this year, darling?" Mom asks.

"Nope."

Margot's not as artistic as Mom and me, and every year she carves words into her pumpkin instead of a face. Usually something from one of her favorite books.

"Which quote?" Mom asks.

"It's from Mary Shelley," Margot says. "*Beware; for I am fearless, and therefore powerful.*"

Dad blinks. "That's heavy."

"Amen," Mom says with a wink.

"That going to fit on the pumpkin?" Dad asks.

Margot shrugs and swivels the pumpkin around. "Maybe I'll just write the word *power*. It can still represent the whole quote."

"Good idea, honey," Mom tells her.

I turn back to my werewolf and add the finishing touches to the outline of his face, his fur, his teeth. I then attach the high-speed carving bit onto the edge of the Dremel and slowly drag the metal tip against the pumpkin's skin, peeling back the top orange layer until a werewolf starts to emerge in its place. By the time Mom, Dad, and Margot pick up their Dremels, the entire kitchen sounds like a dentist's office, the buzzing noise filling the space as we work. Once my werewolf has the basic shape, I attach the sanding band and start to smooth out and thicken the edges in strategic spots, adding texture and depth. When I'm about finished, I pick up the knife again and saw a hole into the moon, so that the candle will have a spot to shine through fully.

"You ready yet?" I ask.

"One more minute," Mom says.

"I've been done. Check it out," Dad says, spinning his pumpkin around so that its goofy, one-toothed, lopsided grin is facing us.

"How original," Mom snorts, shaking her head.

"Dad, that's the same face you carve every year."

"Not true! I added eyebrows. Look." He points proudly to the two uneven triangles positioned above the pumpkin's eyes.

I throw my dad a very sarcastic thumbs-up sign, but in truth, I always love his silly faces: it's been a Jones Family Tradition ever since I can remember.

"Done!" Mom says, spinning her own pumpkin around to reveal a carbon copy of the bride herself. She even used a sander on parts of the hair in order to give the iconic style some texture.

"Well, now you're just showing off," Dad says.

"Mom, that's amazing," I gush, leaning in closer to get a better look.

"Margot?" Dad asks, nodding toward her pumpkin.

On cue, Margot shows off the word *POWER*, which is scrawled in thick, splintery letters across her pumpkin.

"Nice," Mom says approvingly. She looks at me. "Your turn, Marion. Come on, spin her around."

I push my werewolf across the table, and Mom and Dad simultaneously shriek with delight.

"Calm down, you're both so embarrassing," I say, feeling myself blush as I tug the pumpkin back. "It's really not *that* good."

"Oh, stop it. You know it's good," Dad says, leaning over for a fist bump. "Besides, what are you embarrassed about? It's just us."

Margot snorts. "For now."

"Shut up!" I blurt out.

Dad looks back and forth between us. "Did I miss something?"

I say, "*No!*" at the same time that Mom and Margot say, "*Yes!*" Dad blinks, waiting for one of us to explain.

"Marion has a friend coming over tonight," Mom finally says.

"Oh yeah?" Dad asks, his eyes widened in genuine interest. "Who?" He snatches another cookie from off the tray.

"Just a friend from school," I tell him.

"Does this friend have a name?" he asks, taking a large bite out of the side of the skull.

"Tyler," I finally say, bowing my head under his gaze, pretending to fix the handle of my Dremel.

"*Tyler*," Dad repeats.

"Honey, you're sweating," Mom tells him.

"Can you both be cool?" I beg, feeling my heart beginning to beat faster. "It's not even a big deal."

Dad waves me off. "Of course I'll be cool. I *am* cool." Then he looks at me. "Do I still get to watch the movie with you?"

"Eww, no, Dad, that'd be weird," Margot tells him.

"They're having a *marathon*," Mom says.

"Like, multiple movies?" Dad asks. "How late is this kid staying over?"

"I already gave permission." Mom smiles. "This is a good thing. The cards said that a transformation was coming. Maybe they were hinting at a friendship."

Finally. That's what she so obviously wants to add but doesn't. I bristle at the relief on her face. Was I some kind of freak before, or something? Just because I didn't invite people over?

"Come on," Margot says sharply, ending the conversation. She stands up. "Let's go put these outside."

"Yeah," I say, joining her. "My first client will be here soon."

"Honey, I—" Mom starts, but I'm already at the door. I walk outside and place my werewolf pumpkin on the front step next to Margot's.

Mom approaches from behind, cradling her own pumpkin. "Baby, I'm sorry," she says quietly. "I don't want you to think that I—"

"It's fine. I'm fine."

"No, Mar, it's not fine. I mean, I know you have friends at school..."

I brush past her. "I've got to clean my room before the first appointment gets here."

Margot flashes me an empathetic look before I make my way inside and storm up the steps to my room. Once alone, I shut the door and breathe.

She doesn't mean it, I tell myself. *She's just looking out for you. She doesn't think you're a loser...*

Well, maybe not now, I think, *but did she before she knew about Tyler?*

I sigh and collapse onto my bed. I don't have time for this; my first client will be here in fifteen minutes. Enough moping—I've got to clean. Without skipping another beat, I start to bustle around my room, sorting clothes, making my bed, putting books and records back in their proper homes. By the time I light my favorite pumpkin-scented candle and place it in the windowsill, Mom is knocking on the door.

"Come in."

She approaches tentatively, her face bowed. I soften at the look of her, at the weight of her love.

"Mom, I told you, it's cool." I make my way toward her. "We're cool."

"Do you promise, Mar?"

I nod and she pulls me in for a hug.

"I just worry about you," she says. "It's been forever since I've seen you hang out with anyone, and I just thought . . . But I'm just happy you're making friends." She squeezes me a little tighter. "Even if it is with a random kid from art class."

"He's not random," I say before I can stop myself.

Mom pulls away, her eyes wide and bright. "Is he *more* than a friend?"

"No!"

Mom raises an eyebrow. I pick up a dirty sock from my laundry pile and toss it at her. She laughs and throws it back at me. In an instant, we both start digging through my unwashed T-shirts and start chucking them at each other, laughing as we go.

"Umm, hello?" a voice calls, followed by a polite knock against the open door.

Mom and I freeze mid-throw. It's Kat, my first appointment. Dad must have let her in downstairs, but we were too distracted to notice the doorbell.

"Kat—hi." I feel my face grow warm as I scurry around the room, picking up the strewn laundry.

"Welcome," Mom says, piling the clothes into her arms, ready to carry them to the laundry room and out of sight. "Can I get you some cider or a sugar cookie? Home baked!"

"Some cider would be great," Kat says, stepping farther into my room.

"Coming right up!" Mom says a little too enthusiastically. She mouths the words *I'm sorry* to me before tottering out on her heels, taking my dirty laundry with her.

"Cool room," Kat says, looking around. "It's not what I pictured. It's pretty."

I never know whether to take that as a compliment, but I assume that's how she meant it, so I smile. "Thanks." I nod to the workshop door. "Want to get started?"

"Sure." She smiles warmly, exposing two rows of perfectly straight white teeth. "I'm really excited for you to turn me into a witch," she tells me as I lead her into my studio. "You did my friend Lani's makeup last year—she was a skeleton with purple hair. Do you remember her?"

"How could I forget?" I say, thinking back to the bright skeleton with the rainbow tutu. "Can you pull up your hair for me?"

Kat takes a seat on one of the stools and pulls a band over her long waves.

"I'm just going to take a look at your skin," I tell her, coming in close to inspect her color, texture, and pores. "Is it sensitive at all? Do you have any allergies to certain products or makeup?"

"Nope. Nothing."

"Do you have anything on your skin now? Like lotion or foundation?"

She shakes her head, and I start digging through my drawers to find the prosthetic pieces labeled KAT JACKSON: a bent nose, a pointy chin, and a furrowed brow, all of which have been pre-painted lavender.

"Wow, are those mine?" she asks. "I love the purple!"

"I think it's the perfect color for your skin tone. And your dress is gray, right? Purple and gray really complement each other."

"I didn't know that," Kat admits. "I'm pretty bad at art. Mrs. Anderson is always telling me that it's OK to take risks, but I don't know what she means. It's the only class that I have a B in instead of an A."

I pour some toner onto a cotton ball and clean the areas of her face that I'll be applying the prosthetics to. I can tell that Kat is a talker—she wants to chitchat, but I never know what to talk about besides makeup. Luckily, Mom comes in with the apple cider.

"Here you go. Better drink it up now before you get your chin glued on." She hands the cup to Kat, who takes it gratefully and drains it in one go. Mom takes the empty cup back and smiles. "Thirsty, huh? Would you like another?"

"No, thanks, Mrs. Jones. I know Marion has people coming in after me. We should probably get started."

Mom nods and comes around to help me position the first piece: the brow. She holds it while I adjust the placement as needed. Then I apply the glue with a small, flat brush, and together we hold and press the edges until it's firmly in place.

"Looks good," I tell Kat.

"Is this going to hurt when I take it off later?" she asks.

"Nope. We have a kit packed up for you with directions. And you can text me if you have a problem, but I really don't think you will."

Mom and I continue to work until all three prosthetic pieces are glued on, and then I load up my airbrush with the same shade of lavender that I used to pre-paint the pieces.

"This might feel a little cold," I tell her, spraying a few test puffs onto my own arm. "Ready?"

She nods, and I get to work blending the pieces with her skin, until everything is the same shade of lilac. I then switch canisters for a burnt-tan color that I use to shade the cheekbones and the brow line, before finishing the entire look off with a shimmer of silver. Mom adds a swipe of peach to Kat's lips, and I pull her hair out of the ponytail so that it falls back over her shoulder.

"You look magical," Mom says. "Here." She turns the mirror around so that Kat can see herself, and Kat immediately gasps, her eyes widening.

"Oh my gosh. Is this me?" She reaches out to touch the glass. "This is amazing! Marion, you're a genius!"

I blush, feeling a little swell of pride. "Try not to touch your face," I tell her, helping her out of the chair. "Would you mind standing by the white wall for a picture?"

"Sure! Would you take one with my phone, too?"

"Of course," Mom says, taking Kat's phone and motioning for her to stand in front of the wall. "Now do your witchiest face," she tells her.

Kat needs no convincing to launch into character, and we get some great shots before Stella arrives to pick up her own witch's nose.

"You look amazing," she cries, taking in Kat's makeup. She turns to me with panic in her eyes. "How am I going to be able to do *that* by myself?"

"Here, I'll show you," I say, motioning her over to my workbench.

"Thanks so much, Marion," Kat says, leaving her money on the counter. "Will I see you at the dance?"

"No. But have fun."

"Here, I'll show you out," Mom says, ushering her from the room so that I can focus on Stella.

I pull out the spare prosthetic nose and a baggie with the adhesive, a couple of Q-tips, and instructions, as well as the makeup remover for after the dance.

"It'll be best if someone helps you apply it," I tell her. "You just hold the nose against your face and lift section by section like this. Then use the Q-tip with a little bit of glue, and then press and hold. Repeat all the way around until it's secure."

"That doesn't seem so bad," Stella says, shrugging. "How do I get the color to match?"

"Well, I pre-painted it green, so you need to get some green Halloween face paint—the kind you can buy at the drugstore will work fine. Then blend it all over your face and the prosthetic."

Stella takes the bag and hands me a ten-dollar bill. "You're the best, Marion. Thanks for squeezing me in last minute."

"No problem. Good luck."

She breezes out with her bag just as Mom leads my next client in. This is how the next couple of hours go: client after client, application after application. First, we lay a series of gashes and wounds that don't take very long. Then there are a few zombies, witches, and vampires. One goofy pumpkin. A creepy clown. An alien. Mom and I lean over them one at a time, applying the prosthetics with glue, and then spraying the rest of the skin so that the pieces blend seamlessly. We take photos of them all. My heart is humming by the time a text comes in from my last client of the night, Lex, saying that she's really sorry but her crew is running ten minutes late.

"You know what that means," Mom says with a smile. "Cookie break!" She dashes from the room, motioning for me to follow behind.

Together, we make our way to the kitchen, where Dad is already waiting.

"Did I hear it's a cookie break?" he asks, poised near the stove.

Before anyone can respond, Margot bursts into the kitchen, waving Winston around in her hand. "Not funny," she says, slamming the face down onto the counter.

"Hey!" I cry. "What were you doing with Winston?"

Her eyes flare. "What was *I* doing with him? What were *you* doing putting him in my room? Were you trying to scare me?"

"I didn't—"

Margot's scowl cuts me off. "Whatever. Just keep your monsters out of my room."

"What's going on?" Mom asks.

"Nothing," Margot mumbles. "Marion was messing with me. But it's fine."

"I swear I wasn't!"

Dad just smiles. "Did it work? Did she get you?"

"Never," Margot says. I notice a small smirk on her lips, melting the tension in the room.

Mom looks her up and down. "Is that your costume, honey?"

"No way," Dad says, answering for Margot. "Those are just her normal clothes. Except for the glasses. Did you get glasses?"

"I'm *Velma*," Margot tells him, tugging on the ends of her burgundy skirt. "From *Scooby-Doo*. Shivali is going to be Daphne."

"Want me to do your makeup?" Mom asks. "You can be a vampire Velma?" She swipes a tube of red lipstick from off the counter and holds it out to her.

"No way," Margot says, ducking back. "It'll ruin my whole look."

Mom sighs, waving the tube in the air. "You sure?"

"I'm sure." Margot pulls her bag over the shoulders of her puffy orange sweater. "I'm off. See you later."

"Be home by ten," Dad tells her.

"Ten thirty!"

"Ten fifteen, and not a second later."

"Ugh. Fine." She kisses each parent on the cheek and offers me a wave from across the room. "Bye!" She exits through the side door.

No one comments that Margot's curfew is earlier than mine tonight. Everyone is so desperate to have me make a friend that the rules don't seem to apply to me. It's embarrassing.

"Come and have a cookie," Mom says, dropping the tube of lipstick back onto the counter.

"I'll take one upstairs," I say, grabbing a cookie from the tray. "I just want to clean up a bit."

Mom nods. "Sounds good, honey. I'll let you know when your next clients show up."

"Don't work too hard," Dad adds.

"Yeah, right," I snort. "The hardest makeups are still to come."

"You'll do great, kiddo."

He then leans over and clinks his cookie against Mom's. "Cheers," he says with a wink.

I leave the two of them like this, their eyes locked in a smile, as I make my way upstairs.

Back in my workshop, I place Winston on his stand, and then I start to organize my supplies. I line up each prosthetic piece for my last four clients: Lex, Zoe, Kaylee, and Quinn. I feel Winston's eyes on me as I clean.

"What's your problem?" I ask him. The mask glares back at me in a way that sends a shiver down my spine. I swear his smile looks bigger from what I sculpted. And for a second, his hollow eyes seem to glow.

You're being ridiculous, Marion . . .

I turn him around, so that the back of his head faces the room, and with this I continue tidying up. Mom left her playlist running, and I turn it up, singing loudly as I work.

All of a sudden, a familiar voice starts howling along. "*I see, a bad moon ris-ing . . .*"

I spin around and drop my paintbrush on the floor. "Tyler!" I gasp, placing my hand over my heart to catch my breath. I reach out to shut off the music, my eyes shooting over to the clock on the wall. "But—you—you're early."

He smiles that extra-wide smile of his, both his dimples showing. "I wanted to get a picture of you in action."

"In action?"

"Yeah, you know, working. It's for the paper." He pulls out his phone. "Is that cool?"

I immediately begin swiping at my hair, trying to smooth it out. "I'm a mess," I tell him, taking note of my paint-splattered clothes.

"I think you look great." Tyler grins again. "So can I?" He aims his phone at me.

I nod, my head swimming with his compliment. *I think you look great.*

He snaps the picture just before Mom pokes her head through the door.

"You kids want some cookies?" she asks.

"Homemade!" Dad adds, nudging himself in after her. They both stand awkwardly in the frame, holding out a plate of skeleton cookies, cheesy smiles on their lips.

"Oh, yes, please," Tyler says. He accepts a cookie and takes a giant bite. "Whoa, this is amazing!" he says.

"Thanks." Mom smiles at him. "I didn't realize the movie marathon was starting so early."

"He's here to take a picture of me for the school paper," I explain. "Then he'll come back later for the movie."

"Well, why don't you stand in front of the white wall?" Mom asks.

Dad's eyes brighten. "Yeah, want us to help?"

"We're OK, thanks," I say, ushering them out. "Thanks for the cookies." I take the plate from Dad's hand and close the door behind them. I turn to Tyler. "Sorry about that."

"Don't be. They seem cool—way cooler than my parents," he says. His eyes widen, zoning in on the corner of my desk. "Whoa," he gasps. "Winston!" He darts over to the mask, whose menacing eyes are once again locked onto mine.

My heart stops. "Wait. Did you just touch that?"

"Nope. I didn't know if that was OK," Tyler says.

"But I had it turned around. It was facing the back." Once again, I feel the goose bumps prickle my arms.

"It looks so *real*," Tyler says. "Can I pick it up?"

I hesitate, my eyes scanning the creature on my desk as if daring it to move, or wink, or smile. Nothing. I shake it off and snap the rubber band against my wrist a bit harder than normal.

Cool it, Marion.

"Yeah," I finally tell Tyler. "Here, let me get it."

He stands close to me as I pull Winston off the foam head; to my relief, it feels like lifeless rubber in my hands—the same two hands that sculpted it and painted it.

It didn't move, I tell myself.

"This is brilliant! I can't believe you made this," Tyler gushes. "I mean, I *believe* you made it, because you're awesome, but . . ." He blushes, which causes me to blush. "You know what I mean," he finishes, looking away.

"Do you want to try it on?" I ask.

He puts his phone down. "Obviously." He frowns. "But will it fit over my hair?"

I laugh. "Let's try."

"I don't want to break it."

"You won't. The plastic is really durable. Here, I'll help you."

I reach up to get the mask over his head and gently tug the mask down, tucking in Tyler's hair as I go. I'm so close that I can smell the piney scent of his flannel shirt. My stomach does a little flip, and then Tyler disappears and is replaced by Winston. My Winston. My crush wearing my creation.

"It's hard to see in this thing," he says, his voice slightly muffled in the latex.

"That's because it's made for my head, not yours, so the eyeline might be a bit off."

"Do I look scary?" He holds up his hands to mimic a monster about to grab somebody.

"Very scary," I tell him. "Come on, let me take your picture by the wall."

"OK, but seriously, I can't see. Can you walk me over?"

Before I can answer, he reaches out and grabs my hand; our fingers lock as I guide him to the white wall. I'm almost thankful that he can't see my face and how excited I must look. If this were a movie, this would be the moment when we'd confess our feelings for each other. But it's not a movie, so instead, I clear my throat and step back to aim my camera.

"Strike a pose," I tell him.

He immediately puts his hands behind his head, pretending to sunbathe. In the next one, he stands in first position like a ballet dancer. We take a few silly shots before he waves me over to him.

"Come on, let's take one together."

"Really?"

"Yeah, come on!"

I join him in front of the white wall, and I hold out my phone to take a selfie. "Say Winston," I tell him, and he wraps his arm around my shoulder just as the picture snaps. He leaves his hand there for a moment, and I can feel him studying me through the mask. For a second, the rubber seems to fade away, morphing with his skin so that it looks as if they're one and the same—that Tyler has actually *become* Winston. In a flash, Tyler's warm brown eyes appear cold and serpent-like—inhuman. I shiver and reach for my rubber band.

"OK," I tell him, trying to keep my voice even. "Maybe we should put Winston back so that you can see again."

My shoulder feels cold when he moves his hand, and together we lift the monster off his face. He shakes his head, looking dazed. His eyes seem different—yellowish for a moment. *Trick of the light,* I tell myself before turning away. Tyler follows me over to the workbench, where I place the lifeless mask back onto the foam head.

"Check out the moon," he says, gazing out the window.

I join him in front of the glass. "Wow, it's actually red."

"That's why they're calling it a *blood* moon."

"A Super Blue Blood Moon," I correct, watching him as he looks up at the sky wearing a thoughtful expression. Something's changed since before he put on the mask, like his energy's depleted.

"You OK?" I ask.

He shrugs. "Yeah, I'm fine." His eyes remain fixated on the moon. I squint, trying to catch a hint of yellow again, but they just look like their regular brown.

I want to say something, to bring us back into those minutes before he tried on Winston, but my throat is dry—I can't find the words.

"Do you want to do the interview?" I finally ask.

Before he can answer me, there's a knock on my bedroom door.

"Hello, hello!" someone says, pushing through before waiting for me to say *come in.*

The spell is broken in the room, and I feel Tyler jump

beside me. We both turn around and come face-to-face with Lex, Zoe, Kaylee, and Quinn.

"I'm so sorry we're late," Lex says. "Should we drop our coats on your bed?" She nods to the door.

"Sure," I tell her, breaking away from Tyler so that I can properly greet my clients.

"Blame this one," Lex say, throwing a look to Quinn. "Track practice went over."

"It's not my fault!" Quinn protests. "Blame Coach."

"It's cool," I tell them, suddenly feeling very cramped in this small space: I'm not used to having four clients in the studio at once. "Who wants to go first?"

"Ooh, me!" Lex says, shooting her hand up.

"Do you want to wait in my bedroom?" I ask the others. "You're welcome to watch something on the TV in there."

"Cool," Zoe says, motioning for the other girls to follow her.

Lex takes a seat in the makeup chair, spinning herself around like a little kid, talking the entire time. ". . . and the dress I got is perfect. It looks just like the one she wears in the picture . . ."

"I brought snacks," Mom says, entering with a fresh plate of skull cookies. "We all good in here? Tyler, you want another one?" She holds out the plate to Tyler, who still stands shyly by the window.

"I'll take one," Lex says, swiping the biggest one from the tray before Tyler can answer.

I make my way over to him. "Sorry," I whisper. "But . . ."

Oddly, he doesn't answer.

"Hey, what does this do?" Lex asks, pulling my attention toward her once again.

I spin around in time to catch her playing with my airbrush. "Please don't touch that," I say, hurrying to take it out of her hands. "It's kind of delicate."

"I always wanted to try out one of those things . . ." Lex continues to talk and talk, even as I clean her face with the cotton swab, even as I line up her prosthetics and get the glue ready.

"OK, sweetie," Mom tells her gently. "It's important not to talk as we apply the pieces or else your face will look misshapen."

"I definitely don't want that, Mrs. Jones," Lex says, pretending to zip her lips.

"Do you have a picture that we're supposed to work off of?" Mom asks.

Lex hands over her phone, a photograph already pulled up. Mom's eyes widen. "Seriously? You are going to your dance dressed as the old people from Goodie Lane?"

"It's genius, right?" Lex asks.

Mom shrugs. "If you say so. I mean, they are quite glamorous, aren't they?"

"Oh, I know, especially Bea," Lex says. "But Quinn called dibs on her," she adds with a scowl.

"Which one are you?" Mom asks.

"Mrs. Brown," Lex says, pointing to the woman on the end of the photograph, whose face is ghostly white with pinched skin that almost looks like clay.

"What a severe-looking woman," Mom says.

I glance over at the picture, comparing my premade prosthetics with Mrs. Brown's spiked cheekbones and squared jawline.

"I'm ready," I say, holding up the first piece for Mom to place. "You ready?" I ask Lex.

"More than ready." She pretends to zip her lips again.

I stifle a laugh as Mom fits the nose against Lex's skin. Then I go in with the adhesive. By the time the pieces are all applied and I look up, Tyler is gone. He didn't even say goodbye—which is weird enough, but didn't he need to snap some pictures of me working and get that interview? I freeze for a moment, listening to see if he's gone to talk to the kids in the other room, but I only hear the faint hum of the TV. *Did I do something wrong?*

"Honey?" Mom says. "I think we're good. You ready for paint?"

Her words jostle me back into the moment. "Sure," I say, and together we get back to work.

CHAPTER 6

The four makeups take about two hours to complete, which kind of feels like a personal record.

"You all look fabulous," Mom says, ushering the girls over to the white wall. "Let's get a few pictures before you go."

Mom's right: they do look great, if I say so myself. Elderly makeup is one of the most difficult special effects to pull off, but since there's something unnatural about these older women and the stiffness of their wrinkle-less skin, the makeups that Mom and I created look uncannily realistic. Together, we built shadows underneath the eyes, adding a few creases along the hairline and around the lips. Their features are all slightly exaggerated: foreheads a touch too long, cheekbones too severe.

Quinn's look is especially on point, with her black wig teased into a beehive hairdo, and her long satin dress and gold jewelry that she borrowed from Lex's mom. Looking back at the photograph of the real Bea, I'm proud of the work that I did on Quinn's face: her diamond-shaped cheeks jut out in the same place, her chin is pointed, her nose slightly curved. I painted a putty-like base across Quinn's skin, and Mom did a heavy beauty makeup on top, complete with winged-tip black eyeliner and red lips. Something about Quinn's look has a dangerous edge to it, just like the real Bea does in the photograph. I can't quite pinpoint why or what it is, but it sends chills down my spine. When I first spun the mirror around, Quinn herself looked like she was staring at a monster.

"*Are you OK?*" I asked her.

"*It's just so real,*" she answered, touching the edges of her face.

"*Come on, nothing to be scared of,*" Mom said gently. "*It's just some old-lady makeup.*"

"*Bea's not a regular old lady,*" Quinn said, her voice breathy and uneven.

"*What do you mean?*" I asked.

"*Never mind,*" she said, turning away from the mirror.

I study her now over with her friends, posing for Mom's camera. Lex, Zoe, and Kaylee have a relaxed look about them, being silly, jutting out their hips, pouting like the women they're emulating. But Quinn appears to be the odd girl out, really just standing there, barely looking while Mom snaps pictures.

"I think we got some good ones," Mom says, putting her phone down on the worktop. "Marion will send them to you."

We then gather the goody bags and pass them out, telling the girls what's in each one.

"Try not to touch your faces," I remind them.

"Can we eat?" Zoe asks.

"Yeah, you just have to be careful."

"In that case . . ." She swipes a skull cookie from the tray. "Cheers!"

I laugh and usher the girls out of the workshop, catching a glimpse of the moon as we pass the window; it looks even redder and more magical than it did when Tyler and I were last gazing at it. I know it's not a star, but I close my eyes anyway and picture Tyler—his eyes, his floppy hair, his smile . . . *I wish something would happen tonight.* The wish feels real enough to touch.

But then the nerves creep up. Tyler left without saying goodbye. What if he doesn't come back at all? I snap my rubber band against my wrist, trying to be positive.

"You coming?" Quinn asks, startling me.

I nod, throwing one last glance at the moon, before following the group downstairs and into the living room, where Dad sits watching an old horror movie and eating candy. Mom swipes the bowl out of his hands.

"That's for the trick-or-treaters," she scolds.

"Trick or treat?" Dad asks.

"Nice try."

I lead the girls past my parents and toward the door.

"Thanks for everything, Marion," Lex says, handing me an envelope full of their collected money. "These came out even better than I hoped."

"You're welcome. I hope you have fun at the dance."

"Yeah, thanks, Mar," Zoe says. "We're definitely going to win that costume contest."

"Do you think the judges will know who we're supposed to be?" Kaylee asks.

Zoe snorts. "They'll at least know Bea. She's such a legend."

"Was," Quinn says. "She *was* a legend."

Zoe shrugs. "Whatever, Quinnie. Just because old Bea left South Haven doesn't mean she's gone for good." Then she turns to me. "Thanks again, Marion. See you at the dance!"

"Yeah, see you."

I don't bother to tell them that I'm not going. Instead, I wave goodbye as they file out, and as soon as they disappear into the darkness, I suddenly feel very, very tired.

"Pizza's on its way," Dad says as I join them back in the living room.

"Good, I'm starving," I say, collapsing onto the couch.

Mom reaches over to high-five me. "You did really great, honey. Your best ever." She kisses me on the cheek, leaving a red smear of lipstick behind, I'm sure. "I'm so proud of you."

I rest my head on her shoulder. "Thanks, Mom."

The doorbell rings and Dad jumps up, grabbing the bowl of candy. "For the trick-or-treaters," he says, flashing Mom a grin.

"It's the pizza and you know it," she calls back before he disappears into the kitchen.

A moment later, we hear him striking up a conversation with the pizza guy. I sit up and dig into the ceramic candy dish—the one Mom keeps on the side table all year long. Today, it's filled with mallow pumpkins. I scoop out a handful.

Mom steals one and smiles. "What time is Tyler coming back?"

I stiffen. "Seven thirty."

"He seems like a very nice boy."

"He is."

I remember how he held my hand, and the way he squeezed my shoulder.

"What are you smiling about?" Dad asks, returning with the pizza.

"The pizza, obviously," I say, grabbing for the box and placing it on the coffee table.

"Are we going to be civilized and eat at the table with plates?" Mom asks, standing up.

"Nah," Dad says. "It's Halloween. Live a little." He puts a slice into her bare hands, and Mom shrugs and sits back down. "And one for you," he says, handing one to me.

I don't even care how hot it is, I take the biggest bite, allowing the spicy tomato sauce and the fresh oregano and garlic to explode in my mouth, my taste buds doing a little happy dance from the homemade mozzarella cheese.

"It's blissful," Mom says, closing her eyes to savor it.

"You got time for a movie, Mar?" Dad asks. "Before Mr. Red Flannel comes back? I could pull up *Cujo*."

"Jeez, Dad. You're obsessed," I tease him.

He grabs the remote. "What can I say? I love a dog story."

"A *rabid* dog story?"

"Four legs is four legs."

"Then can we get a dog?" I ask.

"Nope," Mom answers before Dad is able to.

The doorbell rings again. "Saved by the bell," Mom mutters.

Dad pats me on the knee. "You're up. Candy's in the kitchen." And then he adds in a whisper, "I'll work on your mom about the dog."

"We're not getting a dog," Mom says dryly.

I sigh and make my way into the kitchen, where I find the bowl of candy as promised. I open the door to a slew of little trick-or-treaters, dressed as everything from Disney princesses to creepy creatures and noble warriors.

"You all look great," I tell them, dropping a piece of candy into each plastic pumpkin.

A little zombie gasps at me. "Are you the monster maker?" she asks, her eyes wide.

"I guess, yeah, some people call me that." I smile. "My name's Marion."

"I'm Sam. You did my sister's makeup last year—it was so cool!" She puffs out her chest. "I'm going to be a monster maker when I'm older."

"Did you do your own makeup tonight?" I ask. "It looks pretty cool."

"Really?" She beams. "Thanks!"

A vampire tugs at Sam's arm. "Come on, let's go. Before all of the good candy is gone!"

"Have fun," I tell them.

Sam continues to wave to me even as I close the door.

By the time I get back to the living room, Dad has started *Cujo*, and Mom is on her second slice of pizza. She hands me another one, and together we continue eating and taking turns opening the door for trick-or-treaters.

Once the pizza is gone, I suddenly become hyperaware of the time. Each tick from Mom's antique clock on the wall seems to thud inside my chest, and my eyes watch the minute hand more than my parents watch the movie.

By the time seven thirty comes around, I'm frozen. When the doorbell rings at seven forty-five, I jump up to answer it, and I can't help but look disappointed at the trick-or-treaters at the door.

At eight o'clock, Dad clears his throat.

"Maybe he got caught up at the dance," Mom says.

"Whatever. It's no big deal," I lie, before excusing myself to go upstairs. I ignore the concerned looks that my parents throw each other as I leave.

My phone is on my bed where I left it, and I pick it up and scroll through for any new messages. None are from Tyler. There's just one from Lex with a selfie of her and the other girls at the dance. *You should come!* she wrote.

I toss my phone back onto the bed and begin to pace, counting my breaths, snapping my band until the pressure dissipates: *three, two, one . . .*

I guess I might as well clean up.

I shuffle into my workshop with my Docs barely leaving the floor. It's not actually as messy as I thought, but something feels off. Probably I'm just upset about Tyler. Cleaning will help—it usually does. I begin the familiar dance of rinsing the tools, placing everything in its labeled containers. It's only when I go to rescrub the surface underneath the foam head that I realize what's wrong.

It's Winston—Winston's gone!

My heart races as I dart around the room, throwing things around as I search high and low, in drawers, behind the counter. Then, in my bedroom, I tear apart my bed, my closet, my dresser.

"Mom!" I yell. "Dad!"

Their footsteps thunder up the stairs.

"What's wrong, honey?"

"Are you OK? What happened?"

I can't catch my breath. "Winston—"

"What about Winston? Honey, calm down . . ."

"He's gone. I can't find him!"

Dad silently starts searching the room, looking panic-stricken in the process. Mom stays by my side, wrapping one arm around my shoulder while gently pressing her other hand against my heart.

"Breathe," she whispers, "just breathe."

"I can't find it," Dad says after he's done searching. He scratches his beard. "Do you think somebody took it? One of your clients?"

"No," I start to say, but then I shake my head. "I don't know. Maybe. I mean, no one else was in here . . ." I trail off.

My clients' faces flash through my mind, one by one. But wait—it was still here when Tyler came over. He tried it on. That means the thief would have to be one of the last four girls I made up.

Or Tyler.

"I have to go to the dance," I say, grabbing my coat from its hook behind the door.

"Now?"

"The thief's there, whoever they are. And I've got to get Winston back." I pull my backpack out from under the desk and begin filling it with random things: panic packing. I grab some gum, and keys, and one of my extra goody bags.

"Honey, what's all that for?" Mom asks, not bothering to hide the worry on her face.

I don't answer, pulling the backpack onto my shoulders. I turn to Dad. "Will you drive me?"

Dad exchanges looks with Mom. "Sure, honey. Let me just get my boots." He makes his way downstairs, with me and Mom trailing close behind.

In the kitchen, Mom gently squeezes my arms. "We'll find it, honey. It's going to be OK. Maybe whoever took it didn't mean it. Maybe it was an accident."

I'm near tears as I shake myself free.

"Do you want me to come with you?" she asks.

"No," I say firmly. "It's fine. I can do this."

"Are you sure?" She chews on her bottom lip, something she always does when she's nervous.

"I'm sure."

With this, Dad grabs his keys from off the counter. "Let's go."

I follow him outside and into the truck.

His loud music fills the cabin; Dad makes a move to lower it, but I stop his hand. The noise is kind of comforting. Together, we crawl at about five miles per hour up and down the side streets, watching out for the trick-or-treaters; their glow sticks zip through the air like fireflies as they dart from house to house with pillowcases full of candy. Fabric ghosts line the crowded streets, hanging from the dogwood trees in wispy rows. Pumpkins grin and glare at us as we pass, their candles flickering on the inside. We then turn onto Main Street, and through a break in the trees I'm able to catch a glimpse of Goodie Pond, which seems to glow orange beneath the bloody moon. South Haven has always been magical at Halloween, and this fact isn't lost on me even as my stomach continues to tie itself into knots.

Dad turns down his punk music at the same time that we pass by a house with a coven of animatronic witches, and without the choppy guitar blaring in the background, I can hear their high-pitched cackles.

"Listen, Marion," Dad starts, his voice coming out soft and unsure. "This is kind of delicate, right?"

I look at him. "What is?"

"You know, one of your clients taking your mask. I know how upset you are, but I'm worried you're going to charge into the dance accusing people."

"I'll be calm," I promise him, the acid bubbling in my chest like lava.

"I just don't think it would be a bad thing if you had help." He raises an eyebrow. "You know, from a grown-up. If not me, then maybe a teacher? Or Mr. Howe?"

"The principal?" I shake my head. "No way."

"Well, what's your plan? Do you even have one?" I don't answer, and he sighs. "What are you going to do if it turns out to be Tyler?"

"It's not Tyler," I snap.

"But Mar—"

"Dad, not now."

"OK, but say it *is* Tyler," he continues, "maybe he just meant it as a joke. Kids do stupid things sometimes. *All* the time, actually."

I don't want to talk about this—I can't talk about this.

"Marion—"

I cut him off with a glare. He sighs and shakes his head. Guilt cuts through me as the silence between us thickens.

"Dad?" My voice cracks as I turn to him for reassurance, my fingers trembling.

His jaw is slack, but he clears his throat. "You'll get it back, kiddo." He reaches over and flips off his music in exchange for the local radio station.

The DJ's deep voice continues to ease through the speakers. "And now for the weather. It looks like this total lunar eclipse is bringing some nasty storms to South Haven, folks. Heavy rain, high winds, lightning, thunder, the works. Meteorologists predict flooding along the shoreline, which can affect power and water systems. Everything should be starting around nine thirty tonight, so make sure you get yourselves home safely . . ."

My hand shakes as I shut the radio off. Dad forces a smile that falls flat. I turn back to the window, trying to control my unsteady breaths by snapping my rubber band.

We continue driving down Main Street until we reach the beach side of town. On my right, we pass a tiny airport, the lights glittering from the small planes that line the landing strip, which stretches across a marshy field. Unkempt seagrass reaches up toward the dark sky. This is not trick-or-treat land. Dad can pick up the pace now and drive the truck with a bit of speed, and we reach the rocky shoreline in no time.

The community center is up ahead: I can see the illuminated MERRICK'S BY THE SEA COMMUNITY CENTER sign, flanked by black and orange balloons. *Welcome Rocky Hill!* a homemade banner reads. *Happy Halloween!* The building itself is shaped like a half-moon, with its back pushed up against the sea, which looks angry. The waves are rising and crashing with such force that the ground itself seems to shake.

Dad eases the truck into an empty spot by the door and

cuts the engine. He reaches for his seat belt. "I'm coming in with you."

Thunder rumbles in the distance as I shake my head. "No, you're not. We already talked about this."

"Yeah, but that was before—"

"Before what?"

He shrugs as a streak of lightning slices the sky.

"I can do this. Don't worry. You can go home and help Mom with the trick-or-treaters. Besides, Dad, didn't you *want* me to go to the dance?" I click the button on my seat belt.

"Forty-five minutes," he says. "I'll meet you back here at nine, not a second later. You heard the weatherman." His eyes flicker to the windows. "It's supposed to get pretty wicked out here later."

"Got it." I reach for the door handle, but Dad grabs my hand.

"Good luck, pumpkin. Remember to breathe."

I force a smile. "Thanks, Dad. I'll text you if I find Winston early." I give a small wave before closing the truck door and making my way to the front entrance.

The waves are even louder outside, and the strong wind whips through my hair, threatening to pull it loose from its topknot. Rain starts to spit in cold bursts, so I run the rest of the way to the double doors. I can feel the thud of the bass drum before I even touch the handles, and the beat all but slaps me in the face as I enter the lobby.

It's an old-fashioned building, with yellowish walls and a faded carpet. There are no decorations except for a splattering of posters, the same ones that were hung up at school. The orange, black, and purple papers flutter as I walk toward the ticket table.

"Well, hello there, Marion," Mrs. Anderson says, flashing me a smile. She's sitting alone in front of a cashbox and a roll of tickets. "Decided to check out all of your wonderful makeups?"

"Something like that," I mutter, my stomach dipping.

She extends her hand. "Ticket?"

Suddenly I panic. I don't have a ticket, and I forgot my wallet. "I . . ." My face grows hot, but Mrs. Anderson waves me away.

"Don't worry about it," she says, reading my expression.

"Are you sure?" I ask.

"Of course. Enjoy yourself, OK, Marion?"

She smiles again. I try to smile back. "Thank you."

"Happy Halloween!" she says.

I take a deep breath and continue down the empty corridor. With every step I take, the music becomes louder and louder, yet there's still something lonely and hollow about this hallway. The sound of my boots echoes above the noise. I stop just shy of the door, the vibrations buzzing under my Docs. My heart rate quickens.

I can't do this, I think. *Dad's right—I don't even have*

a plan. And worse, what if it really was Tyler who took my mask? I trusted him. He was one of the only people I ever felt comfortable with. What if he betrayed me? What if he gets mad when I confront him, and he never wants to talk to me again?

I snap the rubber band against my wrist, stalling for time. Tyler's smile swims into my thoughts. I remember the way his entire face lit up in my room, his dimples deepening as he squeezed my hand and put his arm around my shoulder. It can't be him. And with this thought, I gain the strength I need to push open the door.

The room is darker than I expected it to be. It takes a second for my eyes to adjust, and then they dart around, looking for something familiar. In the front is the small stage where the DJ is set up; behind him is a wall of windows that look out to the sea. The decorations are kind of minimal—just some orange and black balloons and streamers. Underneath them is a collection of monsters, kids from school dressed up in colorful costumes, dancing to a trendy song that everyone seems to know except for me. Even the teachers look like they're enjoying themselves, clustered together in the corner, talking and laughing.

I feel my breaths quickening. There are too many people. I'm the only one not in a costume. If this were a movie, everyone would turn at once and notice me. The thought makes me feel sick.

Maybe this was all a bad idea. I snap my rubber band a few more times, trying to figure out what to do. With the last snap, the song changes to a slower one. The crowd parts, and then I see him.

Winston.

No—Tyler. With his jeans and flannel shirt, and my mask on his head. He's throwing his body around in a way that sort of looks like dancing. He doesn't seem to be with any particular group. I don't see his camera or his notebook either, making it clear that he's not here for the school paper. He's just *here*. And it looks as though he's enjoying himself.

Anger seeps into my bones, hardening me, replacing my initial fears.

That's my monster, and I want it back.

My boots lead me forward, squashing fallen orange streamers in their path. I feel bold as I march, my chin up, my eyes narrowed and focused. *I'm actually doing this!*

"Tyler," I say. No answer. I clear my throat and try again, louder this time. "*Tyler.*" Still no response. I swallow and say his name a third time, before tapping him on the shoulder.

Slowly, he turns around. I shrink back. Something's not right. He glares at me through yellow eyes—serpent eyes—that look nothing like their usual brown. There's no warmth in them. Instead, Tyler looks at me with anger. I brace myself, and despite the rapid beating of my heart, I plant my feet.

"You stole my mask," I tell him. I try to sound bold but

worry my words might get lost in between my nerves and the music.

But he seems to hear me, all the same. He steps in closer, breathing too heavily on my face. I think I smell seaweed.

"Marion," he whispers, his voice deeper and somehow raspier, as though he's speaking through pain. He stretches out his arms, mouth twisting into a smile.

I take a step back. My mask shouldn't do that. The latex shouldn't move that way.

"What's wrong?" he asks, tilting his head. "Aren't you happy to see your creation in the *flesh*?"

I don't like the way he says the last word, dragging out the *sh* sound. It makes me shiver even though the room is warm.

"Tyler, I—"

He cuts me off, closing the gap between us again. "Stop calling me Tyler!"

I open my mouth to respond, but before I can get the words out, I gasp. This close, I can see every groove of the mask, lines that I carved into clay and molded with my own two hands. Except . . . the seam where I blended the front and the back of the mask are gone. It's as though the mask has been fused to Tyler's skin. The gills flutter as if they're real. As if he's breathing through them.

"Oh my—" I try to step back, but he grabs my arm.

"Don't you recognize me, Marion?" he asks with a snarl, his lips stretching to unnatural proportions.

I struggle to wriggle free, but his grip is too strong.

"Winston," I breathe.

He nods. "Yes. Winston. Honestly, Marion, was that the best name you could come up with?" The creature sighs.

I look around. Isn't anyone seeing this? But they're all blissfully unaware, dancing around us.

Winston's eyes follow my gaze. "Pathetic, I know." Then he smiles, revealing jagged, pointy teeth. "What do you say we *really* get this party started?"

"No!" I cry, my breaths becoming more and more shallow.

"What's the matter, Marion? Don't like what you see? *You* created me, after all." He steps back, finally releasing his grip on my arm. "And now you get to see me dance."

The moon seems to shine brighter, illuminating his horrid face. A strange light emits from the sea outside. It highlights the yellow in Winston's eyes, intensifying them. He breaks off toward the front of the room. I shiver in his wake, frozen where he left me. I watch in disbelief as he jumps onstage, making a beeline for the DJ's table. It looks like he's telling the DJ what song to play. When he goes for the microphone, the DJ pulls it away. People are starting to notice the scuffle. Mr. Howe approaches the stairs at the base of the stage.

"Hey!" he calls. "You're not supposed to be up here."

Winston spins to face the principal. His green lips

suddenly stretch open, pulling back wider than any human jawline, exposing a hideous mouth that seems to go on forever, like a series of black tunnels lined by row after row of sharp, pointy teeth.

One person screams behind me. It causes a chain reaction, with more and more kids screaming as they turn to face the stage, until it seems like every person in the room is crying out in shock and horror. Except for me: I'm too scared to scream.

I didn't create this, I think, pressing my back against the wall. *I didn't sculpt those teeth, that serpent-like black tongue...*

A cloud of black ink shoots out from the creature's mouth, covering Mr. Howe's left leg and shoe. Mr. Howe looks around wildly, waving his arms.

"What *are* you?" he shouts.

Winston laughs at the question, the cruel sound cutting across the room. Just as Mr. Howe tries to tug his leg free of the goo, Winston spits out another black slimeball—only this time, it hits Mr. Howe directly on his face. A hush falls over the crowd as we watch the dark oil drip down and coat the rest of our principal's body. He goes completely still.

Mrs. Jockers and a few other teachers try to rush the staircase, but they get shot with the same type of ink that took down Mr. Howe. People begin to panic. I get bumped and shoved into a corner as more teachers storm the stage, and a group of students tries to run for the door.

Winston wrestles the microphone from the DJ, who looks too terrified to fight him anymore; in the end, it doesn't matter. Winston inks him, too, freezing him in front of his booth.

Winston then turns his attention to the crowd. "I wouldn't do that if I were you," he warns, pointing toward the door. I notice that his hand is still human.

Maybe he's not a total monster, I think. *At least not yet.*

No one listens to his warning; in fact, they run faster. The temperature in the room seems to rise about ten degrees, and it's becoming even harder to breathe.

When the closest person, Jess Zagha, reaches for the handle, Winston shoots a wave of ink across the room, hitting Jess with a direct shot. The ink splatters and washes over everyone around her, too, freezing them all in place.

"What's going on here?" someone calls, pushing through the other side of the door, bumping one of the frozen kids out of the way. It's Mrs. Anderson. She claws at her cheeks in horror. Winston doesn't even hesitate: he inks her.

"Any other takers?" he asks the crowd with a snarl, the black ink dripping down his face.

The rest of the students cower at his words.

Winston steps out to the front of the stage, his sneakers teetering over the edge as he scans the room. His pointed tongue shoots out, causing everyone to scream, fearing that he's about to ink someone again. Instead, he uses it to lick away the goo on his own face. Like a whip, the tongue snaps up and around his chin and cheeks. Then he retracts his rows of teeth and flashes us a sinister smile.

"Don't be shy. This is a dance, isn't it?" He does a spin, landing on his tiptoes. "So, let's dance!"

With this, he saunters back over to the DJ stand, changing the song to an old-school eighties one, "Let's Dance" by David Bowie. No one moves.

"Come on," he yells. "Show me your best moves!" He moonwalks across the stage, the waves rising behind him through the oversized windows. I can't help but notice how high the tide is, and how red the moon has become, like at any moment it will start dripping giant drops of blood.

I shrink back against a far wall, watching it all from the shadows.

Winston spins around and points toward someone in the crowd. "Dance!" he orders. I recognize the girl in the elderly makeup: it's Kaylee, looking like she's on the verge of tears.

"Come on, dance!" Winston says again. "You don't want to end up like them." He jerks his fish face in the direction of a line of frozen adults; the only thing about them that moves are their blinking, horror-stricken eyes.

Lex pushes through the crowd and grabs Kaylee's

hand, forcing her to sway haphazardly to the beat. Kaylee starts to cry.

"Not good enough," Winston snarls.

Lex moves forward as if to put herself in between Kaylee and Winston, but Winston shakes his head.

"Uh-uh," he says, waving a finger. "She was warned." He launches a blob of ink at Kaylee. She screams, and the goo freezes her face in a look of terror, the black droplets framing her still-open mouth.

Lex steps back, her eyes spilling over. Slowly, she starts to sway again in a really sad-looking two-step, almost as if she's clicking her heels together. *There's no place like home.* Zoe is now at her side, and the two of them hold on to each other. I quickly scan the room, expecting to find Quinn, too, but I don't see any sign of her.

Winston retracts his mouth, hiding the rows of teeth behind his tongue. He puts his hands on his hips. "Now when I say to dance, I mean *dance.*"

He twirls and shakes his hips, and the rest of the room follows suit, leaving Kaylee on the sidelines. My eyes scan the room for others who've been inked: I count Kaylee, five teachers, the principal and the assistant principal, the DJ, and about fifteen other students who had tried to run. I'm the only one not dancing, and it's only a matter of time before Winston notices me again, and then what will happen?

Discreetly, I pull out my cell phone and check the time

on the screen: it's only been ten minutes since Dad left. I try texting him, but there's no service. I've got to get outside somehow, but my eyes follow the row of students who are frozen by the door. As if reading my thoughts, another small group of students makes a run for it. But they don't get nearly as far as the first group. Winston opens his mouth again and shoots the ink mid-spin, and without missing a beat, he continues dancing, closing his jaw so that he can sing along to the pop song blasting from the speakers.

Behind Winston, the waves rise almost to the window, and I remember what the radio said about flooding.

I bet Winston would love that, I realize. *A sea monster drawing the water in.* I glare at the moon, and it seems to wink back, taunting me. My body starts to shake as I realize how trapped we all are.

"Yeah, now we're talking," Winston cries as the next track comes on. "Let's go—shake it!"

I think it's safe to say that we're all shaking.

Breathe, Marion. Breathe . . .

All at once, the room starts spinning, and Winston becomes a blurry green blob onstage, the shimmer of his gills reflecting the spotlight above him. Just as my breaths become even more shallow, I feel hands grab my shoulders, pulling me into the darkness. By the time I realize what's happening, it's too late to scream.

CHAPTER 7

My eyes dart from side to side, trying to adjust to the darkness. It seems like I've been pulled into a kitchen; the metal countertops and cooking pans cast shadows against the walls.

"My bag—where's my bag?" I ask.

"It's safe," comes a male voice somewhere in front of me. I hear a rustling, as if the person is going through my things.

I reach out my hands, trying to feel around. "Who are you? What do you want?" I can hear the panic in my voice.

"I can't see. I need a flashlight," the boy says.

"Use your phone," a girl answers.

"But it will drain my battery!"

"Ugh, you're impossible. Here, just let me . . ."

Their voices sound familiar.

"Who are you?" I ask again.

A beam of light suddenly cuts through the blackness, blinding me. I hear footsteps.

"Please," I beg, even though I don't know who I'm begging, or for what.

The beam is lowered, revealing my captors: Quinn Parker and Mike Warren.

I sigh, my whole body falling with relief. "Oh, thank goodness. I thought—"

"How are you doing this?" Quinn whisper-yells, her eyes fierce as she shines the light in my face again like I'm in some kind of interrogation room. She's still dressed like Bea, but her makeup is smudged, her beehive is out, and her satin gown is tied up on the bottom with rubber bands.

"Doing what?" I ask, snapping my own rubber band against my wrist.

"Controlling him!"

I shrink back from her glare. "I'm not—"

"I know that's your mask, Marion. I saw it at your house. How do we stop it?"

I feel tears starting to run down my cheeks, the steam fogging up my glasses as Quinn comes closer to me. "I don't know!" I sob.

"Hey, Parker," Mike says softly, placing a hand on her shoulder. "Lighten up. I think she's telling the truth."

"How do you know?" she asks him.

"Come on. Just look at her." With this, he hands me back my bag, and I take it warily.

Quinn squints at me, waiting for me to explain.

"Look," I tell them, swiping away my tears. "That is my mask. I think Tyler took it. But I swear I don't know how this is happening. I don't know how he's—how it's . . ." I trail off, at a loss for words.

"How it's *alive*," Quinn finishes, finally lowering the phone light.

"I told you—I don't know!" The tears fall even harder, my breaths becoming harder to regulate.

Quinn's face softens. "Hey, hey. It's OK. I believe you. I'm sorry. I wasn't trying to scare you."

Mike steps in closer, his eyes barely visible under his Yankees hat. For the first time, I notice his costume: a black T-shirt with a rubber bat duct-taped to the chest. Its wings flap every time he moves. "Hold up—that's *Tyler*? Tyler Dash? The goofy kid from the newspaper?"

"He's not goofy," I say before I can stop myself.

"Tyler?" Mike snorts. "Didn't he dress up like a taco to protest the fake meat in the cafeteria's taco bar? He's most definitely goofy."

I remember that day clearly: the way Tyler's hair poked through the top of the taco shell as he bounded through the lunch line, handing out copies of the Rocky Hill paper, the headline reading: *Justice for Tacos!*

"I don't know," I lie. "Maybe."

"He's in a few of my classes," Mike continues, nodding. "He's hilarious."

"Well, not right now he's not," Quinn says.

Mike shrugs. "I mean, he kind of is. Did you see those dance moves?"

"Mike. Be serious."

"I am serious."

Quinn shakes her head. "Whatever. Funny or not, we need a plan."

"A plan for what?" I ask.

Quinn blinks at me. "To take out Tyler."

Mike laughs again. "I still can't believe it's Tyler . . ."

My heart speeds up, beating in time to the music from the next room. *I wonder what they're doing in there. Are they all still dancing? Has anyone else been inked?*

"We can't hurt him," I say frantically. "Tyler's not really like that." I pull at the rubber band again: *four, three, two . . .*

"What are you doing?" Mike asks, nodding to my wrist.

I feel my cheeks grow warm, but I continue snapping the band regardless. "It helps," I say softly.

Mike asks, "*How?*"

"Leave her alone," Quinn warns.

"Sorry—I don't get it," he says. "How can that possibly help? It looks like it hurts."

It does hurt, I want to say, but I don't answer. I just ping the band again, the pain sending a sting up my forearm. Only, it's not helping. The darkness of the kitchen feels like it's closing in on me.

Think of your strategies, Dr. Magesh would say. *Focus your mind on something. Pick an object in the room and stare at it. Count backward from ten.*

I choose the phone flashlight as my focus object, a beacon in the darkness. *Ten, nine, eight . . .*

But it doesn't work. The room starts to spin beneath me, and I taste the acid burning in my throat. Leaning forward, I place my head between my legs, but the motion only makes me feel sicker. My arms start to tingle, causing the tips of my fingers to become slightly numb.

Stop it, Marion, I tell myself. *Use your strategies: ten, nine . . .*

"Hey," Quinn says. Her voice seems to quiver as she reaches out and touches my arm. "You OK, Marion?"

I try to answer, but my breaths are too uneven—I can't get a big enough gulp of air. It feels like something is pressing down on my chest, and in this moment, I'm terrified that if I fall down, I'll stop breathing.

"I think she's hyperventilating," Mike says. "Or it's some kind of panic attack."

"Marion?" I feel Quinn tugging on my sleeve, but she looks distorted—I can't quite make out her features. "Mike, what do we do?"

There's terror in Quinn's voice, but the sound of my sharp breathing is louder. I need to get up—I need to get out of here.

Abruptly, I stagger across the kitchen, dropping my bag on the counter before dragging my boots to a side door.

"Where are you going? Where is she going?"

"I don't know—follow her. I have to find a paper bag . . ."

There's the sound of shuffling behind me as the beam of light tries to follow my twisted path. I feel for the handle.

"Marion, no!"

I yank open the door. A heavy curtain of rain pounds down so hard that it almost hurts, and the wind is causing garbage cans to roll across the parking lot. I only manage to get in one painful swallow of sea air before a tide of water rushes forward, knocking me down to the concrete floor. Waves lap over my body, the freezing water causing my limbs to shrivel and retract into a ball.

Two sets of hands tug at me just as I become convinced that I'm going to drown.

"Hey, hey, we got you!"

"Hurry up—close the door!"

Mike and Quinn drag me back into the darkness, shutting the heavy door behind us. Together, we all try to catch our breath.

"Here, use this," Mike says, his voice low and hoarse. He hands me a brown paper bag.

I take it, and on command, I make concentrated inhales and exhales, the bag crinkling with the pressure. Someone drags over an empty food crate, and I perch on the edge until my breaths get under control again. Quinn holds the lit-up phone with one hand and rubs my back with the other.

"Stay with her," Mike whispers. "I am going to check out the dance and make sure that nobody heard us."

He darts across the kitchen and peeks out of the small square window on the door. "Seaweed Breath is still dancing," he reports.

Quinn and I huddle close, listening to the heavy beat pulsing from the next room. Winston's voice bellows through the microphone.

"Move your feet!" he yells.

It sounds like chaos in there: screaming, a thumping bass . . . And it's all my fault. Makeup used to be the only thing that made me feel confident. But now, my creation is hurting people.

I breathe into the soggy bag again, my fingers clenched so tightly that I'm sure my knuckles have turned white.

It's one thing to make fake monsters. It's something completely different to know that they're real.

"What's going on out there?" Quinn asks.

He shakes his head. "You don't want to know."

Quinn rolls her eyes. "Actually, Mike, I do want to know. That's why I asked."

I let the paper bag fall to the floor and look back toward the door. Mike's still peering through the window, his face illuminated by the colorful strobe lights shooting out from the DJ table. For a moment, I just focus on the soft purples and yellows, pretending that the cries from the other side are sounds of joy instead of terror.

"It's getting worse," Mike tells us, breaking the fantasy. "Seaweed Breath is inking anyone who tries to escape." He grins. "I got to say, though, I'm not mad about Mrs. Rosch getting slimed."

"Mike!" Quinn scolds.

He blinks innocently. "What? She's the worst. She gave me two detentions last week . . ."

My mind whirs. I try to rise to my feet, but I'm still unsteady, and Quinn has to pull me back down onto the crate.

"We have to get out of here," I say.

"Did you not hear me?" Mike asks. "I literally just said that he's inking anyone who tries to make a run for it."

"But what about that door?" I ask, pointing toward the loading dock exit.

Mike comes over to the two of us and folds his arms across his chest. "That didn't work out so well for you last time, did it?"

"He's kind of right," Quinn says. "The storm is too

strong out there. Besides, where would we go even if we did escape?"

"To—to get help," I explain. "To get the police."

"Police?" Mike laughs and hops up onto the counter behind him, letting his feet swing against the side. "Yeah, good luck with that. Cops are useless."

Quinn says, "Hey! My dad was an officer, remember?"

"Of course I remember. He was a great man. But that doesn't mean you trust the others. They didn't help at all last time."

"Wait a minute, what?" My fingertips are tingling with fear or rage, or a combination of the two. "Has this happened before?"

They exchange looks. "Umm . . ."

I blink. "This *has* happened before?"

"No, not exactly."

I fold my arms, unconvinced. "Explain."

Quinn stands up and joins Mike at the counter. "It's not what you think. We really don't know anything about what's happening to Tyler."

I eye her. "But?"

"But." She takes a breath. "We may have dealt with other supernatural stuff before."

"Like *what*?" I try to control my volume, but it doesn't work.

Mike jumps down and stands beside Quinn. "We vanquished some demons."

My mind is spinning faster than the room. "Some?" I cry. "Some—as in—*more than one*?"

"A handful."

"Who?"

"The ladies who lived on our street a few months ago. And then also our old neighbors on Goodie Lane." Mike pretends to do a slam dunk in an imaginary basket. Then he turns to me. "Didn't you wonder about the costumes?" He motions to Quinn.

It all suddenly makes sense—Quinn's reaction to the old-age makeups, the way she looked at herself in the mirror as if she was seeing a ghost. I pull myself to my feet, ignoring the wave of dizziness that follows. "So, you're telling me that Bea and the rest of them were *demons*?"

Quinn shrugs one shoulder. "I mean, I guess technically you'd say that Bea was a witch, right? And Abigail was a ghost."

Mike nods and then puffs out his chest, flashing a cocky smile. "But don't worry, Marion. They didn't stand a chance against this." He flexes one of his biceps. I'm too stunned to laugh, but Quinn faces off against him.

"Oh, because *you* defeated them all by yourself?"

"I mean, I guess you helped a little," Mike says, a smirk on his lips.

"Then how come I won the bet—*twice?*" Quinn asks.

"You were just lucky," Mike tells Quinn.

"Oh, really?"

"Really."

"Then why don't you put your money where your mouth is? Again?"

Mike laughs. "Now?"

"Yeah, now. Third time's the charm." Her eyes twinkle as she speaks, as if this is some sort of game instead of a life-and-death situation.

"What are you two talking about?" I ask.

"We always do this," Mike says. "It's kind of our thing."

"Can't it be *your thing* another time?" I demand. "Or make a bet about sports like normal people?"

"Don't worry, we'll be quick," he says. "You'll be saving your boyfriend in no time."

"He's not my boyfriend," I mutter, looking at my feet.

"Oh yeah, he might not forgive you after this whole thing," Mike agrees, nodding his head toward the door. "I know I wouldn't."

"Mike," Quinn says through clenched teeth.

"What? It's true! If you made a mask that turned me into a monster, we'd be done, Parker."

My hands start to shake, and I try to steady them against my knees. The floor starts to shift beneath me, and I have to lean against the countertop; the cold metal steadies me as

I take deep, deliberate breaths. *Ten . . . nine . . . eight . . .* I tell myself to focus, to stare at the sheen in the metal and to count the drumbeats pounding from the next room.

"Don't worry. I'm never making another mask again," I say.

Quinn frowns. "Don't be ridiculous. This isn't your fault. And you're so good. I mean, check me out; I look just like Bea." She frowns. "At least I did, before I messed it up."

"You still look like Bea. I actually hate it," Mike says. "I keep thinking that she's come back from the dead to reclaim Goodie Lane."

Quinn scoffs. "Not a chance. We destroyed her power source, remember?" Then her face turns serious. "That's what our bet should be about, right, Mike? The power source. I say it's the moon."

Mike shakes his head. "Nope. It's definitely the makeup."

I cringe at his words, even though they could very well be true. I remember my earlier wish on the moon: could my dream for "something to happen" have backfired? Mom told me that makeup is magic. Could she have been right? Could I really have caused this terror?

"It's not the makeup," Quinn argues, causing me to exhale a small sigh of relief. Then she holds up her hands, gesturing to herself. "If it was, then why haven't I turned into a monster?"

Mike laughs. "You really want me to answer that?"

She shoves him playfully.

"Ow! Easy, Parker, I need these muscles."

Quinn rolls her eyes, but before she can answer, a blood-curdling scream erupts from the dance hall.

CHAPTER 8

The three of us dart over to the door and peek through the kitchen window, keeping our bodies wrapped in shadow. The lights from the ballroom cause my eyes to sting, and I realize that I have no idea how long we've been hiding in here.

Winston is still onstage, but he's no longer dancing. He's pacing back and forth, his arms flailing around.

"Oh my gosh, look at the water," Quinn whispers.

Mike and I follow her gaze toward the back of the room, where the sea crashes against the large picture windows.

"It's going to break through . . ."

For a moment, I'm hypnotized by the sound and the force of the waves, and I become very aware of the destruction that they can cause if they manage to get in. Some kids on the dance floor appear to be having the same fears: many pairs of frightened eyes shift between the windows and the monster. No one's dancing anymore, and that seems to be upsetting Winston.

"You bunch of ingrates!" he cries, his voice booming. He paces faster, his sneakers pounding against the stage floor as he moves. "Is it too much for me to ask for a little cooperation here?" He spits ink as he talks, so that small bursts of black oil splatter onto the kids near the stage. Some of them become paralyzed, but it depends on where the ink lands. If it's on their skin or their hair, they're doomed. But if it lands on a costume or a wig, they seem to be OK so long as they don't panic and accidentally smear it over their face or hands.

But most of them panic. Most of them are in trouble.

"Dance!" Winston yells, stomping his feet like a toddler. "That's all I want. It's not that hard, is it?" He juts out his chin to look around the room. "Is it?" Black ink flies out of his mouth as he shakes his head. "No! No, it's not." It coats the row of dancers in front of him, freezing them in place with their mouths open in horror.

"Just dance!" Winston shouts, black spit drooling down the front of his flannel shirt.

Mike whistles under his breath. "That boy is *losing* it."

The word *boy* causes me to gasp. "Do you think Tyler is still in there? I mean, do you think that he's OK under the . . ." I let my voice trail off, afraid of the answer.

"Probably not."

Quinn glares at Mike as my stomach tightens. "Don't listen to him," she tells me. "Of course Tyler's OK." She pauses for a second. "At least, I *think* so."

I stiffen, refusing to believe that Tyler is lost forever inside that sea demon. Every horror movie I've ever seen shows a way to defeat the monster. Usually, it has to do with taking down whatever brought the creature to life. Like the Wolf Man—he only turns into a beast during the full moon. Maybe Mike and Quinn could both be right with their bet. I mean, it *is* a lunar eclipse, and this particular one looks especially sinister. I remember how weird Tyler got in my room when he was staring at the moon, like he was hypnotized by it. Come to think of it, he hadn't seemed the same ever since he tried on Winston.

"Maybe we just need to unmask him," I wonder out loud.

Mike grins and points at Quinn. "Ha! It's the makeup, see? I win the bet!"

She shakes her head. "It can't just be the makeup. Or else everyone Marion touched would be a monster."

Mike steps over to my side. "Tell her, Marion."

"I mean, I'm not positive," I admit, feeling nervous with their attention on me. "But maybe you're both right. Maybe it's the moon *and* the mask."

"*Both* right?" Mike frowns. "So you're saying we tied?"

"There's no such thing as a tie in a bet," Quinn tells him.

"One of us has to be *more* right than the other." She looks at me. "Right, Marion?"

I ignore all mention of their stupid bet. "Can we just stay focused?"

"Yes, right," Quinn says. "Totally focused. Finish what you were saying."

"But—" Mike starts. Quinn nudges him to shut up.

"Maybe," I continue, "if we pull the mask off before the eclipse finishes, the spell will break. I don't know if it will work, but I think it's worth a try."

Mike jumps back. "Wait, *spell*? Why are you talking about spells?" His eyes widen. "Don't tell me *you're* a witch like Bea."

"Not that I know of," I mumble, remembering Mom's words: *"There's magic in makeup."* Then I look back at him. "No, Mike. I'm not a witch. I wish I knew why this is happening, but I don't. I'm sorry."

"Don't be sorry," Quinn says. "It's not your fault."

"I mean, it kind of is," Mike says with a shrug.

"*Mike!*"

"What? I speak the truth."

"Do you need a snack or something?" Quinn asks him. "Because you always lose your filter when you're hungry."

"Why? You got food?" he asks hopefully.

"No," she admits. "Where would I hold a pack of gummy bears in this stupid dress?"

"Then why did you *offer*?" Mike cries.

I hold up a hand, cutting them off. "He's right—it *is* my fault," I say. "And that's why I have to be the one to unmask him."

Mike raises one eyebrow. "You sure about that, though? Don't take this the wrong way, but you don't really strike me as the hero type."

"Mike," Quinn growls. "I swear to—"

"I think I should do it," Mike says, ignoring the rage in Quinn's eyes as he interrupts her. "Just tell me how. Because that mask looked like it was part of Tyler's skin, so I don't know if we can just pull it off."

He's right: when I was up close to Winston, I couldn't even see the seam. At this, I turn back to the window, pressing my face against the cool glass. Winston is dancing again, another 1980s pop song blaring behind him. The crowd shimmies along, but their faces look worn and defeated, and there are so many more people dripping in ink and frozen in place, like figures in a wax museum.

"It has to be me," I say. "I don't know why, but my instincts are telling me that I'm the only one who can stop him."

Quinn puts a hand on my shoulder; it startles me at first, but when I look to her, her face is kind with understanding.

"If there's one thing I've learned from living in South Haven," she says, "it's that you have to trust your instincts. Come on. Let's make a plan."

She leads us back farther into the kitchen. We pull three empty food crates into a little circle to sit in, our heads pulled in close together with Quinn's phone perched between us, shining a light in the space. I snap the rubber band against my wrist in time to the music in the other room.

"Marion, there's something you should know," Quinn says, flashing me a guilty look.

My body stiffens. "What?" I don't think I can handle any more surprises tonight.

"I saw Tyler at your house," she starts.

I remember Tyler standing in my bedroom, leaning against my workshop counter with an easy smile on his face as Quinn and her friends barreled in. But then it was like he disappeared: I didn't even see him leave.

"And?" I ask, pressing Quinn to continue.

She starts to tug on her dress, wringing it between her fingers.

"Quinn." My heart beats faster. "Did you see him with the mask? Did you see him take it from my room?"

"Yes," she says, expelling the word in a sigh.

Mike looks at her. "Seriously?"

"I just saw him holding it," she says. "But he definitely wasn't wearing it yet."

"Did you talk to him?" I ask.

"For like a second. I told him I liked the mask and asked

if you made it for his costume, but he just kind of nodded. He seemed really out of it."

"I didn't make the mask for him," I tell her. "He stole it." The word *stole* gets caught in my throat for a minute.

Quinn frowns. "I thought you said he was a nice guy."

"He's obviously not who she thought he was," Mike says.

"Tyler isn't like that," I say, gesturing toward the dance happening next door. "The real Tyler is . . ." I search for the right word. "Sweet."

I pull out my phone and scroll through the saved pictures until I land on the one of Tyler posing in front of my white wall. I hold the screen out for Quinn and Mike to see. "Look. He wore the mask earlier. But it wasn't a part of him—you can still see the edges. You can see his eyes—his real eyes." I swipe past the photo and land on the selfie of the two of us, with his hand squeezing my shoulder. I look ridiculously happy in the picture, and it makes me hate the mask that I spent months creating even more.

"You have service?" Quinn asks, motioning to my phone.

I check and shake my head, before shoving the phone back into my pocket.

The bass continues to thud in the next room. I can't help but think about all our classmates holed up in there, and the thought makes my legs start to twitch, itching to make another run for it.

Quinn suddenly gasps, shining the flashlight onto the floor. Water has seeped in somehow, forming puddles underneath our shoes. Her eyes widen with terror. "What's happening? Mike?"

Mike holds up his hands. "I don't know—why are you asking me?"

Quinn kicks the water at his ankles. "Because you're the science genius!"

Mike kicks the water back. "So?"

"*So*, this isn't supposed to be happening! Tides don't rise this fast."

I can feel my heart racing as the weight of the water sloshes against my Docs. I look back toward Quinn and Mike, and for the first time since dragging me into the kitchen, they look scared.

Quinn kicks the water again. "It has to be the moon," she insists.

I turn to Mike, remembering how smart he was in social studies class—and apparently that's not even his best subject. "Is she right? Could it be the moon?"

He shrugs. "Maybe. Supermoons can cause the tides to rise, yeah, but this—" He stomps his feet in the water. "This is next level. It's almost . . ." He trails off, as if thinking of the right word.

"Supernatural?" Quinn finishes.

"I didn't say that," he snaps.

"Really?" Quinn asks. "After everything we've been through, you still can't say the word *supernatural*? What part of that ink-shooting monster out there looks natural?"

"I prefer the word *phenomenon*," Mike says.

She sighs, softening her tone. "Come on, Mike. You know everything there is to know about space. Think. What's so special about this lunar eclipse?"

Mike plays with the rubber bat still duct-taped to his shirt. "It's called a blood moon because of the color."

"Yeah, I think we guessed that," Quinn says. "But *why* does it turn that color?"

"Because Earth is directly between the sun and the moon."

"How long does it stay that way?"

Mike twists his lips as he thinks. "I think I read that it lasts a little over an hour—at least the part when the moon is fully in Earth's shadow."

I do the math in my head, trying to remember how long ago the moon looked this red. "If you're right and it only lasts an hour, then we're seriously running out of time."

"But that's only if the moon is what changed Tyler," Mike says.

"It has to be," I tell him. "It must have changed my mask into something—I don't know. *Magic*."

I jump up and make my way over to one of the small back

windows. Mike and Quinn follow close behind. Together, we peer through the glass: the moon is scarlet, casting an eerie light over the water, which has risen so high that it's now crept up to the loading dock and is pushing against the door.

"That's impossible," Mike says. "It's rising too fast!" He moves over to the door and tries the handle; it won't budge.

"We're trapped here," I realize, hearing the panic in my own voice. My breaths become sharper with each inhale; I need to slow them down. *Ten ... nine ... eight ...*

"How is it all connected?" Quinn wonders. "The moon, the water, Winston ..."

"Finfolk," I realize suddenly.

"This isn't really the time for homework," Mike tells me.

I turn away from the window, looking at him. "Don't you see? That's what Tyler's become. You researched them, too. Remember what happens? The shape-shifter takes captives back into the sea and holds them hostage forever."

Mike purses his lips. "What are you saying?"

"Winston can't take a room full of hostages to the sea," I tell him, "so he's bringing the sea to them."

Quinn gasps and steps closer to Mike. He squeezes her hand. It's easy to see that there's something between them. A warmth, a protectiveness, even in spite of all the bickering and banter. Something twinges in my chest. *Guilt?*

No. *Envy*? Maybe. It's no secret that I don't have a lot of friends, but Tyler was starting to become one of them. What if he never gets changed back and walks into the sea? Then he's gone forever.

"We've got to stop him," I say, clenching my fists at my side, trying my hardest to look brave even though I don't remotely feel it. "Before he and everyone else drowns."

I wait a beat as Quinn and Mike glance at each other, seeming to have a silent conversation. Finally, they both nod and let go of each other's hand.

"Let's do a head count—see how many others have been inked," Mike says.

He leads us to the other end of the kitchen, where we can squish together and peer through the small window. Winston is no longer onstage.

"Where is he?" Quinn asks.

"I don't see him," I tell her, my pulse racing as I scan the crowd. Our uninked classmates are still dancing, little waves splashing around their feet. Their faces are full of panic.

"The water's gotten in," I whisper, my heart beating faster in my chest. "It's starting to flood in there, too."

But where's Winston?

Suddenly, a hand slams against the glass. We scream, ducking down in the dark.

"What was that?" Quinn whispers.

"*Shh*," Mike tells her.

Together, we press our backs against the door, straining our necks to peer up. The hand is still there, and I can also now see the cuff of red and black flannel.

"It's him," I breathe.

"*Mar-ion,*" Winston sings. "Come out, come out, wherever you *are*!" He shouts the last word, slamming his fist against the glass.

I scream, and he laughs. His face is now peering through the glass, trying to scope us out in the dark. Quinn grabs my hand; I squeeze it back.

"*Mar-ion.* Can you come out and *pla-ay*?"

My whole body is shivering. *What if he finds a way in? What if he inks us and drags us into the sea? What if my monster destroys us all?*

Quinn grips my hand harder; Mike is holding her other one. I squeeze my eyes shut, trying to concentrate on my breathing. When I reopen them and chance a look up, I see Winston's nose—the nose that I had spent hours trying to get right—pressed against the glass.

"I'm waiting," he taunts. "Time's almost up." With this, he opens his mouth, showing a menacing row of pointy teeth. His tongue whips out, and he shoots black ink all over the window.

He then turns his attention back toward our classmates. "Let's go, party people!" he shouts, his voice sounding farther and farther away.

"Is he gone?" Quinn whispers.

Mike nods. "Think so."

He's the first to stand and try to peer through the window, but it's completely coated in goo.

"Can't see a thing," Mike whispers. "But I'm pretty sure he's gone." He motions to us on the floor. "Come look."

Quinn jumps to her feet, but I hesitate where I am, my limbs still shaking.

"It's OK," Quinn assures me. "He's not here anymore." She extends her hand, and once again, I take it, allowing her to pull me up.

Together, we try to peer through the ink, but it's useless.

"We have to open the door," Mike says.

"What? That's a terrible idea," Quinn tells him.

"It'll be fine. I'll just open it a little bit." With this, Mike reaches for the handle, pushing the door open a crack. The music seeps through, the sound ten times louder than it was when we were barricaded in the kitchen. Winston, thankfully, is back onstage, dancing and shimmying around.

"The water is even higher than it was before," Quinn points out. "Look at how soaked everyone is."

Kat Jackson is the first person I notice, holding up her witch's dress as the water splashes around her calves.

"We're going to drown! Let us out of here!" she cries.

Her fear is spreading to a small group of girls who hike up their skirts and pants as they wade around in the water; together they trot in circles, bumping into each other and screaming.

"Stop *screaming*," Winston warns, still wiggling to the beat.

But Kat can't stop, her beautiful lavender face twisting with each cry. She looks like a painting that's been splashed with water before it dried, and the mascara from her eyelids causes black ripples to drip down the sides of her cheeks. She makes a run for it—straight for the exit. She's quicker than I would ever be running through water in heels, but unfortunately, Winston is quicker. He shoots out a spray of ink, coating her entire body in the oily substance, paralyzing her before she can even reach the door. Her friends scream and run toward her, but Winston shoots them as well, freezing them all, before licking the residual liquid off his fangs with a pointy black tongue.

"Anyone else want to try and leave?" he asks, taunting the crowd. "Have a go! I'll give you a head start. Look, I'll even close my eyes." He dramatically covers his monstrous eyes with his hand—Tyler's hand—and he starts counting down from ten. I hold my breath with each number, but not one person moves.

"One!" Winston opens his eyes and looks around. "Wow.

You lot are smarter than you look." He spins on the toes of his Converse. "Now, dance!"

I hear a ripple of cries and sniffles as people slowly begin swaying to the beat again, too terrified to really dance, but even more scared to stand still. Winston retracts his teeth before falling into a split onstage. I allow the door to fall closed in front of me, and then I step back. Quinn and Mike peek their heads out one more time, watching the chaos from within.

"Are we too late?" Quinn whispers.

Mike shakes his head. "I don't think so, but we don't have long. Maybe twenty minutes or so?" He frowns at the monster spinning around the stage. "Man, that boy *really* can't dance."

"Give him a break," Quinn snorts. "He's got a whole new head to get used to."

A head that I built, carved out the gills, carefully molded the eyes, tried on again and again to make sure it was just right . . .

"That's it!" I tell them.

"What?" Quinn asks.

I think back to my bedroom, when I had to guide Tyler over to the white wall. "The mask wasn't made for him. It was fitted for me. When he tried it on in my workshop, the eyes didn't match up to his, and he couldn't see very well."

"You sure about that?" Mike asks. "Because he seems pretty capable of shooting that ink on target from across the room."

"But he has no peripheral vision," I insist. "Maybe we can sneak up on him? You know, from the side?"

Together, we study Winston as he twirls, nearly toppling over onstage.

"She may be right," Quinn says to Mike.

"Maybe," he says. "But we need a diversion either way. I need to be able to get close enough to him to lift the mask."

I feel my heart practically beat out of my chest. "I told you. It has to be me."

Mike gives me a look from beneath the brim of his hat, but he doesn't say anything.

I turn back to the dance and watch Winston move for another minute, noting the fast rush of the water now pulsing through the room. At this point, every single chaperone has been inked, and there are only a handful of kids left who haven't been paralyzed. And Winston's still dancing, his limbs swinging around in awkward rhythms, his head too large for his body. The scene would almost be funny if it wasn't sohorrifying.

"Someone should get up there," Mike mutters. "Show him how it's really done."

Quinn's eyes widen. "That's it! A dance-off!"

Mike raises an eyebrow. "What are you talking about, Parker?"

"Just hear me out. He's been trying to get people to dance since he got here. If the three of us—"

"I'm not dancing," I quickly say.

"You have to."

"Nope, not doing it. I'll unmask him and do whatever else you need, but I can't dance in front of people."

"Marion, don't be ridiculous," Quinn tells me.

"No, I think she's being serious," Mike says. "I saw her stage fright in action in language arts the other day. I had to save her."

"You didn't *save* me," I tell him, anger creeping into my voice. I feel myself grow hot. "You made me nervous. It was your fault I froze."

Mike ignores me and turns to Quinn. "Looks like she's going to need me to save her again," he says with a smirk.

I know what he's doing: I know he's trying to goad me into agreeing to get onstage, and it sends a spark of fury through me, making me want to be brave.

"Fine," I tell them both before I can change my mind "Fine. I'll do it."

Mike and Quinn give each other a subtle high five before Mike turns back to the window. "We're coming for you, T-Monster."

Quinn raises an eyebrow. "You've named it?"

"Of course I did. T-Monster for Tyler Monster."

"That's not his name," I say. I watch my creature dance through the water, splashing against the stage. "His name is Winston." The red flannel spins and spins until all I see is a blur.

CHAPTER 9

We get to work in the shadows of the kitchen. We keep the lights off to maintain our cover as we sit on the crates and plan.

"If Winston catches us before the dance-off, we're done for," Quinn says.

"Well, we may be done for no matter what," Mike replies.

I have to say that I've come to respect Quinn and Mike's combined ability to stay cool in the face of danger. They seem to approach demons the same way I approach makeup: like professionals. In some strange way, they must be rubbing off on me: my hands haven't tingled since I made the decision to help them stop my monster.

"I'll take the lead in the dance-off," Mike offers, raising his hand as if we're in school. "I'll challenge Ty—I mean Winston."

"But he could ink you," Quinn says.

Mike snorts. "He'll have to catch me first. I'm a track star, remember?" He pretends to run in his seat, zigzagging his arms like the Flash. "Just make sure the song is a good one. If I'm going to get inked, I at least want to go out in style."

We put our heads together and begin throwing around song ideas, which is easier said than done, especially for me. I mean, which record is best to thwart an evil sea monster who's possessing my crush's body?

"It's got to be something poppy," Quinn says. "You know, something with energy."

Mike starts to rattle off a list of modern songs, but none of them feel right. I like Tyler, but he's not *that* cool. He's definitely more of a vintage soul.

"Eighties," I tell them. "The song's got to be from the 1980s."

Mike scrunches up his face. "Are you kidding? That's so *old*."

"Trust me," I insist, the confidence rising in my voice. "He'll be way more into that than any of the songs you've been suggesting."

"She's right, Mike," Quinn agrees. "Haven't you been listening to what he's been playing in there? It's been nothing but eighties music since he inked the DJ."

"But *why*?"

I feel myself blush. "Because that's what I was listening to while I made him."

"Fine," Mike sighs. "But it's still got to bop if I'm using it to dance for my life."

Quinn smirks at him. "I thought you said you could dance to anything?"

Mike puffs out his chest. "Of course I can." He then flashes a cocky grin, pointing at the two of us. "You aren't ready for this." His shoulders do a little shimmy, and a laugh escapes my lips.

"Be serious," Quinn scolds him, before turning back to me. "Do you remember what specific songs you listened to when you made the mask? Something Winston might like? Something he hasn't already played out there?"

"I'm not sure," I admit, the pressure building in my chest.

Quinn chews on her bottom lip and exchanges looks with Mike.

"It's fine," he says, adjusting his hat. "We can dance off against any song. It doesn't matter at this point. We just have to get moving."

"It *does* matter," I tell him. "The right song might be able to connect with Tyler—the *real* Tyler. It might unlock something in him that helps us save him."

"But *what*?"

"Here, let me see what I have on my playlist." I pull my phone out from my pocket and swipe the screen to life.

I scroll through the latest list of songs I have saved especially for Halloween. *Dancey . . . dancey—it has to have a beat,* I tell myself.

"What about this one?" I ask, showing a title to Mike and Quinn. They shrug.

"'Somebody's Watching Me' by Rockwell? Never heard of it," Quinn says.

"It doesn't matter," Mike tells her. "Let's just go with it. Look how high the water is getting." He stomps his shoes in the puddle below us. Then he eyes me. "You cool to plug that into the speaker? It's got to be loud."

"I think so."

"Then let's go."

My breath escapes me. "*Now?*"

He kicks water at my Docs. "Well, yeah, before we drown in here."

He's right: The water is rising rapidly now. If we wait any longer, it'll be too late—we'll be trapped in the flood, and Winston will make a break for the sea, taking our classmates with him. Never to return.

"OK," I say as I tuck my phone back into my pocket. "Let's do it."

I start to stand, but to my surprise, Quinn takes my hand. She looks nervous.

"You're sure about the song, Marion?" she asks. Her wide eyes flicker over to the kitchen door, where the bass continues to boom from behind the wood frame.

I nod. "As sure as I can be. Besides, I think Tyler likes eighties stuff, too. We talked about it once in art class."

All of a sudden, Mike smacks his wrist against his forehead. "Oh, wow—it's you!"

"What's me?"

"The girl from art class! Why didn't I think of this before?"

Quinn lets go of me and reaches out, placing her palm on his cheek. "You feeling OK?"

Mike moves away from her. "I'm fine. I just figured out that Marion is Tyler's crush."

Heat runs through my body despite my feet being submerged in ice-cold seawater. "What?" I manage to choke out.

"I'm in math with Tyler," Mike explains. "Last week, I was complaining about art class, and he kept going on and on about how much he liked it, which is stupid because who likes art?"

"I like art," I say. "A lot, actually."

Mike grins. "Well, so does your boy, Tyler. He told me he really likes a girl from his art class, someone he sits next to, someone who helped him with one of his projects."

I know that my face is red even in the darkness.

"Do you sit next to him, Marion?" Quinn asks.

I try to form a response, but all I can manage is a nod.

Mike whistles. "Man, how unlucky in love are you? I mean, what are the chances of someone turning their own crush into a sea monster? Yikes!" He pretends to shiver.

I fall back down onto the crate.

"You can try and be a little more sensitive about it," Quinn hisses at Mike.

"OK, OK, I'm sorry," he tells me, standing up. He holds out his hand. "Come on, we have to go."

I don't move.

"See what you did?" Quinn says. "You shouldn't have said anything."

"No way. If anything, Tyler having a crush on Marion is *more* of a reason for us to move," Mike says. He grabs my hand and pulls me up. "Seriously, Marion. You'll never get a date if your crush gets lost at sea."

I've known Mike Warren for less than an hour, but I already hate it when he's right. And in this moment, he's totally right. Besides, I wanted to save Tyler even before I knew that he liked me back.

He likes me back!

We *need* to save him.

"Let's go," I say, standing up with a stomp in the water, leading my new friends toward the door.

CHAPTER 10

The kitchen window is still covered in ink, so we have to peek through the cracked door. The dance hall is in chaos. Water has risen to the knees of our classmates, their costumes soaked, their bodies visibly shivering as they huddle in groups. Makeup and drugstore face paint are dripping down the sides of their cheeks, mixing with sweat and tears and worry lines. They look worn. I catch a glimpse of Stella Naples in the distance: her nose has been glued on upside down and a little crookedly, and what's left of the green makeup doesn't match the color I'd pre-painted the prosthetic with. She's sobbing so hard that her wig has all but fallen off.

Lex and Zoe hover near a still-frozen Kaylee, as if trying to form a protective barrier around her. I shoot a quick glance over to Quinn and notice her watching the trio with horror in her eyes.

Through the large picture windows, a streak of lightning seems to split the sky in half, illuminating the dance hall and the dark red moon outside. The lights begin flickering like the flame of a candle.

"The eclipse is almost over," Mike whispers. "This is our only chance."

Quinn turns to face us, her eyebrows raised in worry. "What if it doesn't work? What if we can't unmask him?"

Mike squeezes her shoulders, turning her toward him. "Come on, Parker. Have we ever been wrong? We're two for two. Our track record for fighting demons is, like, *flawless.*"

Quinn chews on her bottom lip, considering.

"What do you always tell me?" he asks. "*Trust your instincts.*"

This seems to do it: I watch the haunted look dissipate from Quinn's face, evolving into a hard line of determination. We all stand quietly for a moment, our bodies stiff as we listen to Winston's music blaring.

I look from Quinn to Mike, realizing that in their presence, I don't feel as anxious: my fingertips no longer tingle, and for once my lungs don't swell in fear. For the first time, I actually belong to something important. And so, against all my better judgment, I take a breath and say, "Let's go."

Mike claps his hands, causing Quinn to shush him. She then steals his Yankees hat and squishes it down over her beehive. It looks so ridiculous on her that I can't help but laugh and have to bite my sleeve to keep quiet. Mike swipes his hat back, and Quinn scratches the skin around her prosthetic nose.

"OK, listen, Marion," she says. "I know you're a genius with this special effects stuff, but I really hate wearing this makeup."

I suddenly remember the goody bag in my backpack. "Want me to take it off? I have some remover with me."

Her eyes brighten. "Please!"

"Will it take long?" Mike asks.

I shake my head. "Two minutes."

"Just make it fast."

We shine the flashlight through the dark to find my bag, and I immediately set to work pulling off Quinn's makeup piece by piece. By the time I'm through, she looks like herself again, fresh-faced and young. She throws her wig and jewelry onto the kitchen counter.

"Much better. Thanks, Marion. I just wish I had normal clothes," she mumbles.

I tuck my supplies back in my bag and shrug. "Can't help you with that. I'm not Mary Poppins."

We join Mike back at the door, where he has been keeping watch. I stand back beside him and peer through the crack: thankfully, Winston is still onstage, sloshing through the water, following a beat that he alone seems to care about.

"You ready?" Mike asks.

Quinn and I nod, and together the three of us press all our weight against the kitchen door; even though it's partially cracked, it's still too heavy to open all the way. There's too much water..

"Push!"

We grunt as we move, until finally we fall through to the other side, landing on our knees in the freezing water. It smells like the ocean, like salt and seaweed and summers on the South Haven shore, only without the warmth or the sunshine or the protection of Mom's cherry-print parasol.

Lex and Zoe are the first ones to notice us, but Quinn holds up her hand to them and shakes her head, warning them to stay away. The girls exchange a look but listen. We stumble to our feet and shrink back against the wall.

"I'm going to go get his attention," Mike says. "You both sneak along the two side walls until you reach the stage. When I see you're close, I'll challenge him. Don't worry, I'll be loud enough to keep his attention on me. Then,

Marion, you've got, like, one second to get that song blasting. If you take too long, I'm sure to get inked, and I really don't want to get inked. I *hate* standing still." He makes a face as he looks over to our paralyzed classmates, his brown eyes showing a hint of fear beneath the brim of his baseball hat.

"I'll be quick," I tell him.

Quinn takes a step closer to Mike. "If that thing starts to open his mouth, you run. Promise me you'll run?"

He smirks at her. "Parker, you worried about me or something?"

"Just promise."

"OK, I promise. One flash of teeth and I'm bolting. Happy?"

She smiles at him, stepping so close that their heads almost touch, and for a moment I swear that they're going to kiss. I shrink back in an effort to give them space, but in my awkwardness, I end up splashing both of them with water.

"Oops. Sorry . . ."

Mike turns, the smirk suddenly replaced with his game face. I imagine that this is the expression he wears during track meets. Apparently, he's good—apparently, he and Quinn are *both* good. Rocky Hill's very own athletic superstars.

"It's time," he says, tugging on the brim of his hat.

Without another look back, he breaks away from us and

begins kicking the waves with his heavy, urgent steps, heading straight for the stage.

"Now, go!" Quinn whispers, running to the opposite side, leaving the right wall for me to make my way down so that I can be closer to the DJ's table.

Winston hasn't noticed us yet. Mike continues to weave around the frozen bodies, and it's only a matter of time before my monster catches sight of him. Lex and Zoe watch me with puffed-out cheeks as if they're holding their breath.

So much is riding on this one song, I realize. *I hope I chose the right one, one that will wake Tyler up enough to help us fight Winston.*

My socks are soaked inside my Docs—so are my jeans—and it leaves me shivering as I walk, step by step, quickly enough to make strides but slowly enough to not cause too much commotion. Mike is traveling faster, and the water makes loud clapping sounds as he moves. *Slow down!* I want to call to him. But it's too late: Winston notices him before I'm able to reach the stage.

He stops mid-spin, his head cocked to one side as his yellow eyes evaluate the moving target coming toward him.

"Hey!" Mike shouts just as a bolt of lightning crashes through the window, highlighting Winston in all of his terrifying, scaly glory. The overhead lights flicker and hum, and the song playing in the background suddenly ends.

"Well, well, well," Winston says. "Who do we have here?" He looks Mike up and down.

My limbs are shaking, and my muscles feel like rubber. Every fiber of my being wants to run in the opposite direction, far away from the monster that I created.

But I'm so close—mere feet away from the DJ deck. If I take a few quick steps, I'll be on the stage and can plug in my phone and play the song. Quinn is already on the stairs across the stage, half hiding behind the frozen set of teachers. She nods, encouraging me.

Mike is still charging forward, dodging the human statues in his path. He stares hard at the creature in front of him, who's starting to open his gnarly mouth, exposing the rows upon rows of crisp white teeth and a snapping, serpent-like tongue. I created menace in the mask, but this evil is above and beyond anything I could have sculpted.

Mike lifts the brim of his hat enough to make eye contact with me, his expression pleading. I nod to him. *I got you,* I want to say. I start moving again, making my way up the side stairs. I did it! I've reached the DJ's table. I try desperately not to look at the frozen DJ behind the music stand, his face stretched into a never-ending scream. Across the stage, Winston flashes his black hole of a mouth, hissing at Mike. Mike, to his credit, holds his own and points at the creature.

"You!" he yells over the rain and the waves and the sea of sobbing students. "You think you've got moves? I'll show you moves." He stomps his right foot in the water, creating a splash all around him. "I challenge *you* to a dance-off!"

The crowd audibly gasps, and for a moment I can feel every individual heartbeat drumming through the room.

Play the song! Quinn mouths.

I nod, and my fingers grope around the DJ's table until I find the right cord. Yanking it out, I plug it into the jack on my phone, turning the volume way up, praying that I don't get electrocuted in the process. Thank goodness, the stage is high enough that it hasn't flooded like the dance floor— not yet, anyway. But the puddles are beginning to form, and it's only a matter of time.

There are a few quick hits on a snare drum before a steady, allegro beat fills the air, accompanied by the sound of a keyboard playing in C-sharp minor. The combination creates a spooky rhythm that demands attention. Breathing heavily, I turn back to Winston and watch him stare down his opponent with what seems to be more curiosity than anger.

The crowd disperses into a half-moon shape as Mike tucks his knees into his chest and jumps onstage, landing without so much as a wobble. Thunder booms in the near-distance, but everyone is too hypnotized by the scene to be scared anymore. Something big is happening here—even

Winston seems to appreciate the drama. The creature backs up and holds out his arms as if to welcome his adversary and give him room.

"This is what I'm talking about," Winston says to the crowd. "This is what I mean when I say *dance*."

Mike takes this opportunity to get into the beat. He starts by nodding his head and shaking his shoulders—lightly at first but growing in intensity as the song picks up. Then his chest starts popping, and his arms throw out some shapes as he starts to use the space around him. At the end of the first verse, he spins and points to Winston, before taking a big step backward to give his opponent the floor.

I bite my lip and snap the band against my wrist, praying that Winston won't just ink Mike. I shoot a worried look to Quinn, but to my surprise, she trots out into the center of the stage. *Mic!* she mouths to me. I snatch the microphone off the table and toss it to her; she catches it in one hand, before turning to the audience.

"Come on, everyone. Give it up for Winston!" she cries, clapping enthusiastically.

Mike flashes her a shocked look, but immediately he seems to understand. His face turns into a grimace, and he shakes his head at the monster. "I'm not worried," Mike tells the crowd, strutting back and forth. He juts out his chin toward Winston. "Fish Face over here can't beat this." He starts to flex his biceps, hamming it up.

Winston's mouth appears to open wider, clearly not appreciating the heckling.

Quinn, thinking quickly, turns to Winston, holding the microphone near his oil-stained black tongue. "Are you going to take that, Winston? Come on and show Mike what you can do." She pulls away the microphone and turns back to the crowd. "Let's make some noise for Winston!"

I clap meekly from the sidelines. I know I should get in there and help Quinn and Mike, I know I promised, but my Docs are frozen in place. Even though there's a monster standing just a few feet in front of me, nothing seems more terrifying than the two hundred pairs of middle school eyes. Their stares burn into my skin, staining me like Winston's ink. I shake my arms, trying to get the tingling sensation to stop. It doesn't matter that most of the crowd is frozen; I absolutely can't dance in front of them, not even to save Tyler.

Suddenly, the crowd is moving again. Lex pushes her way toward the front, whooping and cheering. "Yeah, Winston!" she yells, jumping up and down. "Let's go, Winston!"

Zoe's close behind, and she launches into an impressive cheerleader routine, complete with a high kick that almost takes out Lex's prosthetic nose.

And this is all it takes: the rest of the Rocky Hill kids follow their lead, baiting the monster with their cheers. Winston can't help himself—he smiles. He starts to clap along to the applause, before retracting his teeth and tucking them away. He accepts the challenge with a twirl, and the crowd goes wild. But as I gaze around the faces, I notice that everyone's eyes remain widened in terror, even as Winston launches into a pretty solid robot, his limbs jerking in a series of mime-like, stop-motion movements. When the second verse finishes, he offers a low bow to his audience, before stepping back and pointing to Mike.

"You're going down," he taunts.

Mike doesn't miss a beat as he flies into a backflip, landing with a flourish that causes puddles to splash around him.

Winston shakes his head as the water settles. He *boos* his opponent with a double thumbs-down, encouraging our classmates to do the same.

Mike almost seems inspired by the banter, meeting the shade with his own high energy. He transitions from the jump into a mini pop-and-lock routine. The rubber bat on his T-shirt flaps with the movements so that it looks as if it might just fly away toward the Super Blue Blood Moon—which, come to think of it, is starting to look less and less bloody as the clock continues to tick.

When I look back, Mike's on the floor, spinning like a turtle in his shell, the water splaying around him. For a moment, Winston looks so impressed that he stops booing, and when I glance over to Quinn, her jaw is practically on the floor. Guess she never saw Mike dance before—or at least not like this.

When the verse ends, Mike jumps back up and points to Winston. Winston shakes it off and takes center stage again and starts doing what I can only describe as the Aunt Janice: the classic two-step snap that my dad's sister does at weddings whenever they play Bruce Springsteen. It's quite possibly the tamest dance move ever, but you'd think he just did a flip or something the way that the crowd is cheering. He ends his turn by folding his arms across his chest and nodding over to Mike.

Mike throws his head back and lets out a loud, exaggerated laugh. "Weak! That was *so* weak."

Winston steps forward. "Oh, you think you can do better?" His mouth starts to open in a snarl, and my stomach clenches as I catch a glimpse of teeth. Quinn, thankfully, jumps forward in between them. She makes two fists in front of her and proceeds to do the worst Running Man dance that I've ever seen. For a moment, Mike and the monster just stare at her, shocked.

"Come on, Winston," she goads.

Winston doesn't waste another beat before he punches out his own fists and starts doing an even more embarrassing version of the dance move. Soon enough, the entire audience is doing the Running Man—well, at least the unfrozen part of it. Winston is so hyped, he drops down into the water and starts wiggling his body up and down with his arms pinned to his sides like a worm. The sight is hypnotizing; I stand still, just watching.

"What are you doing?" Quinn whispers, suddenly at my side. Her eyes remain focused on Winston.

"I—I—"

"You need to get over there and unmask him."

"But I—"

"Look at the moon!"

I follow her gaze toward the window, and it appears like a gray varnish has started to coat the moon's surface, the red fading. Lightning flashes more rapidly now, the bolts mere seconds apart, creating a strobe-light effect throughout the hall.

"Come on!" Mike yells, beckoning me over to the center of the stage.

But my feet won't move. I was ready for this—I *thought* I was ready for this. The plan was mine; the mask was mine—everything was mine. Only now, I feel the doubt start to roll over me. The rubber band snaps against my wrist.

I already tried to confront Winston one time tonight. I tried to be brave, but it only seemed to egg him on. He inked most of my classmates because of me. What if I fail again?

Quinn takes my hand. "Hey, look at me." Her eyes bore

into mine. "You can do this. I know you don't think you're brave, but trust me: you are."

Her confidence slowly bleeds into me, waking up my limbs. My feet break free from the small puddle that now feels like concrete. She offers me a small, reassuring smile, before turning back to the dance-off. Then, a horrified expression takes over her face. I follow her gaze, and see Mike take a dive toward Winston. *He's trying to unmask him!*

"Mike, no!" Quinn yells.

Only her shout backfires, sending a warning to Winston. He spins around just in time, opening his extended jaw, revealing his rows and rows of teeth. His pointy tongue unrolls and shoots the thick black ink at Mike.

CHAPTER 11

"No!" Quinn screams as Mike freezes in place with his arms still outstretched, his mouth open mid-scream.

Winston does a little pirouette and a curtsy for the crowd. It takes them a second, but the crowd soon gets the hint and begin clapping. Winston eats it up, continuing to dance around Mike's frozen body, the black goo dripping from Mike's hat to his outstretched hands, all the way down to his sneakers. Quinn starts to bolt forward, anger radiating off her, but I pull her back.

"You can't," I insist. "He'll ink you!"

"But Mike . . ." She trails off, tears welling in her eyes.

I can't let any more of my friends get hurt. Brave or not, I have to do this. After all, Winston is my monster.

Letting go of Quinn, I take a gulp of air and tentatively

scoot away from the DJ's table. My Docs shuffle through the water until I reach the front of the stage.

"Hey, Winston!" I yell.

My monster turns around slowly, his shoulders raised with menace, his scaly head cocked to one side as if amused by my presence. His jaws start to open again, tongue flicking against his jagged teeth.

Quinn must have turned up the volume, because the music swells as Winston gets closer and closer—so close that I can see every detail of his head and face. All the hours I spent crafting him. *I made you*, I want to say. *And you're beautiful.* In spite of being utterly terrified, I can't help but admire the sculpture of the curves and edges of Winston's cheekbones and gills, and the way the murky colors almost melt into a shimmer, and how his eyes turn down slightly in the corners. "*He looks sad,*" Mom said. At the time, I agreed, but now I see Winston differently. He doesn't look sad; he looks lonely. I know better than anyone how that feels.

But lonely or not, I can't let him get what he wants.

The audience grows quiet in front of us, and suddenly it sounds as if I'm far away from everything, or as if I'm underwater. I hear a muffled sound to my right, and then to my left, and it takes me a second to realize that what I'm hearing is Quinn cheering me on. Then, all of a sudden, the sound comes rushing back into my ears, and I have to close my eyes to take a breath, until finally the song breaks through. It feels as if I'm just coming up for air. I start moving my body to mimic the only dance move that I know: the Arm Swing and Howl that's in the prom scene from *Teen Wolf*.

Step, step, howl. Swing, swing, howl...

I repeat these steps over and over again, until it feels like muscle memory. When I open my eyes, I see the crowd copying my dance moves in the rising water, their arms swinging from side to side like a werewolf with bent claws, their heads thrown back as they pretend to howl at the moon. I feel like I'm in my own version of a teen horror movie, and I can't help but think about how much Tyler—the real Tyler—would appreciate this moment.

I turn toward Winston. He's started to mimic my moves, trying desperately to remain a part of the group. I watch him, trying to find a trace of the goofy smile and the dimples, but all I see is a teenage sea creature whose bobble head leans back to howl at the not-so-bloody moon.

Oh my gosh—that's it! When Winston howls, his neck is exposed. I can see exactly where the scales end and the human skin begins, and even though I can't make out the seam of the cowl, I can tell where it should be. I know my target. I just need to get closer.

I make eyes at Quinn, whose body is still moving in a

ridiculous manner despite her serious expression. She stays close to Mike, dancing around him in a protective circle. I nod to her, and then I start to swing my arms wider, stretching them out toward Winston with every step I take. The water is rushing in now, and I feel it pushing against my legs as I dance toward the right, a little more, a little more, until I'm within reach of my monster.

Winston is too hyped. We've gotten him overexcited. Even though everyone is following his rules, he still sends a spray of ink across what's left of the crowd, freezing them in place. It's just Quinn and me left.

Through the window, the moon shines like a giant iridescent pearl, looking more gray than red at this point, and I know that once it goes completely gray, we're done for. Everyone frozen will be dragged out to sea. Winston will totally take over Tyler's body. I have to finish this now.

Do it! Quinn mouths to me. I take one last side step so that I'm directly beside Winston, my hands close enough to reach out and touch the elbow of his soft flannel shirt. I squint at the slime on the monster's skin, at the way the gills move up and down with his uneven breaths. His eyes aren't the ones I remember gazing back at me in my bedroom.

Tyler? Are you still in there? I try to find a trace of him among the greens and the blues, but all I see is a monster.

My monster.

A sea creature who apparently loves to dance. Winston is so into the song that he doesn't even seem to notice me. My fingers extend. I'm almost there.

Suddenly, though, he stops dancing. The song's fading out, getting softer and softer until it disappears completely, being replaced with my bonus track, my Hail Mary: the theme song to the *Gremlins* movie. Winston freezes when it starts playing. It's like every gill on his body stops moving, as if he's holding his breath. The staccato keyboard fills the room, and slowly, very slowly, he turns and faces me.

"Tyler?" I say, my voice barely more than a whisper. I clear my throat. "Tyler? Tyler, can you hear me?"

There's a flash in Winston's face, and for a second, the bulbous fish eyes seem to change into the familiar brown shade that's warm and human. My heart beats faster, but as fast as the change occurs, it disappears again, almost instantly.

"Tyler's gone," Winston snarls. He grabs my wrist, tugging me toward him, his fingers digging into my flesh. I twist and manage to slip out of his grasp, but in doing so, my rubber band snaps and falls onto the floor.

Quinn leaps into action, trying desperately to pull me away as Winston opens his mouth, exposing the rows of teeth. Since I'm close enough to smell the seaweed on his breath, I can also see how serrated the teeth are, and I imagine how they would feel tearing into my skin.

His black tongue whips out, nearly grazing my cheek, taunting me.

I shout his name. "Tyler!"

Winston digs his nails into my shoulders. "I told you not to call me that."

I ignore him. "Tyler, I know you're still in there! You're funny and kind. And you're my *friend. Tyler!*"

There's a sudden flash of brown in his eyes, another promise of a human heart within. Winston's grip slightly loosens.

I don't hesitate. Before Winston can open his mouth even further, I reach forward, ripping at the scales and frills around his neck where the cowl of the mask should be. I tug upward with every ounce of my being, as Quinn tries to pull me out from under Winston's grasp.

Then the sprinklers turn on, lights turn out, and the room is enveloped in darkness. I feel something, or someone, pulling my arm down to the ground until I'm lying in the water, and then all becomes quiet and still.

CHAPTER 12

The lights flicker back on when the sprinklers turn off. As I get my bearings, the moon is the first thing I see: its surface a radiant gray, without a drop of red in sight.

"You did it," Quinn breathes from somewhere beside me.

Gingerly, I lift my head from the stage to search for her voice. I spot her lying next to me in a puddle, which is notably less deep than it was during the dance-off. In fact, all the water seems to be receding, returning to its home beyond the shore. Mike is at her side, rubbing his eyes; the sprinklers must have washed away the ink.

I sit up and roll toward him. "You OK?"

He groans and stretches. "Think so." He shakes out his limbs. "I feel weird, though. What happened? Did the sprinklers go off? Was there a fire?"

Quinn and I exchange worried looks. "You mean, you don't remember?" she asks.

Mike scratches the back of his neck. "I don't know. It's fuzzy. I remember dancing." He grins. "I'm a good dancer, right?"

I expect Quinn to tease him, but instead she just smiles. "The best."

"I'm glad you're OK, Mike," I tell him.

"Should I not be?" he asks. "Seriously. What happened?"

Instead of answering, I look around. To the left, I see my classmates sprawled out over the dance floor, huddling together and clutching their soggy costumes. Even the teachers are moving again, no longer paralyzed by the thick black goo. The ink has somehow disappeared, just like the invisible ink I used to write with when I used to play detective alone in my room as a kid. Everyone looks confused, and sleepy, and a bit worse for wear. Maybe something about the ink erased their memories? Could it be possible that they won't remember the flood, or the storm, or even Winston?

Winston.

I look down and yelp as I suddenly notice his face clenched between my knuckles. I drop the rubber mask onto the floor, and the empty eyes stare back at me, lifeless.

An arm clad in flannel reaches out for me, and then

Tyler's face—his normal, human face—stretches into a familiar grin.

"Hey," he says, his smile widening so that his dimples press into his cheeks. "You came to the dance after all."

I blink, not knowing whether I should run, or scream, or throw my arms around him in relief.

Tyler sits up, his knees touching mine. "Oh, cool," he says, reaching for the mask. "You brought Winston."

"Are you kidding?" Quinn cries, snatching the mask away from him. She tosses it to me, and I hold it up to the light, turning it over in my hands, looking for a clue, a reason, a hint of magic. But there's nothing.

"Oh-*kay*?" Tyler says, rolling his eyes toward me, as if to imply that Quinn is the one acting strange. Then he looks around. "Hey, why is *everybody* totally soaked? Did the sprinklers go off or something?"

I bite my lip. "Yeah," I tell him. "There was a bad storm. It messed with the power and everything."

"My equipment!" the DJ shouts. He's dressed in a damp tuxedo-printed T-shirt, which has a fake bow tie on the collar. The color matches the purple fedora that's sitting over on the DJ table. He inspects his setup for water damage. "How in the world?" He pushes a few buttons, tugs on a few wires, and within seconds, "Blue Moon" fills the room.

"It still works!" the DJ cries. He flashes a relieved grin before tugging the purple fedora down onto his balding head.

"Worst DJ ever," Tyler whispers, leaning toward me.

Before I can answer, Mr. Howe trots onto the stage, shaking the excess water from his navy suit.

"I'll take that. Thank you, Miss Parker," he says, reaching down to grab the microphone that she's still holding. He clears his throat and signals to the DJ to cut the music. "Blue Moon" abruptly stops in the middle of a verse.

"It appears we've had some minor flooding issues this evening," he begins.

"*Minor?*" Quinn chokes out.

Mike shushes her as Mr. Howe continues.

"Therefore, in the best interest of the facility, and for the safety of everyone here"—he gestures to the crowd—"the administration has decided to end the dance a little early."

"What happened?" someone yells from the crowd.

"Hey, Johnny—did you pull the sprinkler again?" someone else asks.

Laughter ripples through the crowd, until a girl's voice cuts through the giggles.

"Ugh, Johnny. I'm going to get you for this—you've totally ruined my dress!"

A tall boy I vaguely recognize holds up his hands. "It wasn't me, I swear! I was just dancing and then—"

"And then what?" Mr. Howe asks, peering down at Johnny over the brim of his glasses. Johnny is at a loss for words.

"I—I don't remember."

Mr. Howe waves him toward the stage. "I think you need to come with me."

"But it wasn't me this time! I swear . . ."

"Poor guy," Mike mutters beside me.

Tyler snorts. "Poor guy? It probably *was* him! He pulled the fire alarm just last week and rained out the parent-teacher conferences."

Quinn raises an eyebrow at Tyler. "You're one to talk."

Tyler's eyes widen. "Me? What'd I do?"

"Nothing," she sighs. "Let's just get out of here."

Mr. Howe continues to try and settle the crowd. "So, if you could please call or text your parents—"

"But Mr. Howe, it's not fair!"

Groans rise from the audience. The same students who were literally crying to be released not even ten minutes ago now don't want to leave.

Mr. Howe waves them off. "Now, now." He sends a sympathetic smile around the room. "You've had your fun, haven't you? And we can't forget that we have the spring dance to look forward to in May. So, at this time, please take out your cell phones, and give your folks a call to pick you up."

He turns and for the first time notices us all sprawled out across the stage. "Let's get a move on," he orders, waving his hands as if to shoo us away.

"Don't have to tell me twice," Mike mutters, jumping to his feet. He looks at Quinn. "You want a ride? I already texted my mom."

"Your phone's working?" she asks him.

He shrugs, holding up the screen. "Yeah. Why wouldn't it?"

Quinn shakes her head and stands up next to him. "I'll fill you in later."

"Come along, kids," Mr. Howe says again, ushering us off the stage. "It's time to call your parents. Let's go."

"Mr. Howe, wait!" someone calls from the dance floor. It's Lex, cupping her hands around her mouth to be heard. "You forgot to crown the best costume!"

Mr. Howe sighs heavily into the microphone. "Really? Look at you all." He gestures half-heartedly toward the crowd of water-soaked costumes and a trail of lost capes and hats strewn across the floor.

In response, the crowd starts yelling a series of *yesses* and *whoops*. They're so loud that Mr. Howe takes a step backward on the stage.

Mrs. Anderson emerges, joining Mr. Howe. Her ginger hair is wet and tangled, but it's definitely an improvement

over the black oil look she was rocking just a few minutes earlier.

"Can I talk to you for a second?" she asks Mr. Howe. She
pulls him away from us and whispers something to him, at
which he shrugs and then nods.

"It seems," he says, speaking back into the microphone,
"that the teachers were able to tally your votes before the
sprinklers went off. We can announce the winner for the
best costume before your parents come."

The crowd cheers as Quinn, Mike, Tyler, and I stand
awkwardly on the edge of the stage, not knowing whether
we should try to sneak away now or wait until Mr. Howe
is finished.

Mrs. Anderson takes the microphone out of our
principal's hand. "This costume was chosen before the little
flooding issue," she starts, "but I've got to say, her makeup
has only gotten better with the water. Please congratulate
Kat Jackson!"

I start cheering before the rest of the crowd chimes in.
Kat pulls her best Miss America impression, looking both
delighted and shocked with her hand fluttering over her
heart, waving to her classmates as she practically floats
onto the stage. Mrs. Anderson's right: the water has only
enhanced Kat's look. The lavender paint job has become
slightly warped, taking on these cool new shapes that I
hadn't even imagined sculpting, and the streaks of black

mascara give her witch costume an even more ominous effect. She looks beautiful and menacing—a makeup artist's favorite combination.

Mr. Howe takes the microphone back from Mrs. Anderson, telling Kat, "Sorry. The trophy got lost in all of the confusion. But you can still make a speech, if you'd like." He hands the microphone to Kat.

She smiles. "It's OK. I don't need a trophy." She then sets her eyes on me from across the stage. "Besides, if there was a trophy, I would give it to Marion Jones—the best special effects artist in South Haven!"

She gives back the mic and runs over to me, pulling me into a giant hug as the audience erupts with applause. For a second, I freeze, not knowing what to do with my arms; finally, though, I tell myself to exhale, to hug her back, to breathe in the saltwater smell of her still-wet hair. The sound of the applause fills me up from the inside and out.

When we pull apart, Kat is beaming as Mrs. Anderson and Mr. Howe escort her off the stage, motioning for the four of us to follow.

As we pass the DJ, he tips his purple fedora toward Mr. Howe and asks, "Hey, boss? We good to play one more song while the kids wait for their rides?"

Mr. Howe purses his lips before nodding. "Sure. Can't hurt, can it? Just one, though."

"You got it." Then the DJ holds up my phone. "Oh, and is this yours?"

"It's mine!" I cry, darting forward just as he starts to scroll through my still-open playlist.

"Good track. I think I'll play it," he says with a nod, dropping my phone into my hand.

What track? I want to ask, but before I can even form the words, a familiar snare drum taps its way through the speakers. I feel Quinn's nails dig into my arm.

"Seriously?" she asks him.

The DJ just closes his eyes and begins to dance behind his table.

"Keep it moving, kids," Mrs. Anderson says, and the four of us trot down the stairs, spilling onto the dance floor, where our classmates shake it for one last number, not seeming to remember the last time this song was played.

Lex, Zoe, and Kaylee call Quinn over, waving and jumping like three giddy friends at a regular, non-life-threatening school dance. Quinn nods at them before throwing her arms around me, squeezing tightly.

"We did it," she whispers, pulling back and smiling at me. She then tugs on Mike's arm. "Come on. I want to say goodbye to them before your mom gets here."

"Please be quick," Mike tells her. "I really can't stand this song."

"I kind of like it," Tyler says, shaking his shoulders to the beat. He looks at me. "Want to dance?"

"No!" I say, perhaps a little too quickly.

Tyler stops shimmying, looking slightly hurt. Before I can say anything, my phone buzzes in my hand: it's Dad.

Outside, the message reads.

Coming, I type back.

"My dad's here," I tell Tyler, tucking my phone into my pocket. I grip Winston with my other hand. I'm suddenly very tired. Even so, it's hard to leave Tyler this soon. In a way, it feels as if we just got here.

He bites his bottom lip and looks up at me from beneath a mass of curls. "I guess it's probably too late for our movie marathon, huh?"

"Yeah, I think so."

His face falls a bit, looking sad in a way that reminds me of the lonely look that Winston had. My knees weaken at the sight.

"Marion, did I do something wrong?" Tyler asks, his voice cracking a bit. He seems nervous to hear my answer.

Be brave, I tell myself. *Tell the truth—or at least part of the truth.*

"You stole my mask," I say.

Tyler's eyes widen. "Me? No, I never . . ." He trails off, his brows furrowed. "I—I can't remember. *Did I?*"

I nod. "That's why I had to come here. You stole it from my room. Quinn saw you. I think you were trying to use it for a joke or something."

The color drains from his face as he processes my words. He opens his own mouth to speak, but nothing comes out. I want him to say something to make everything better, to take the sting out of the night. But he remains silent, and I feel my phone buzz again in my pocket.

"I have to go," I say. "My dad is waiting."

Tyler nods, running a hand through his hair. He still looks shell-shocked. "I'm so sorry, Marion. I really don't remember doing that, but I—"

"It's fine," I cut him off. "I know you didn't mean anything by it. Night, Tyler."

Our eyes meet, and we gaze at each other for five full heartbeats.

"Good night, Marion," he finally says.

With this, I make my way to the kitchen to grab my backpack. After stuffing Winston inside, I head back toward the yellow corridor. It's now buzzing with students on their phones, talking to one another in clumps.

When I push through the double doors, I expect to be greeted by rain and thunder, but instead the sky is clear, the silver moon illuminating the now-calm sea. The tide has already receded, and there's no trace of prior flooding. In fact, the only evidence of the storm is the homemade

Halloween Dance banner, now twisted up on the pavement like a discarded napkin.

Dad's truck is parked in the same spot where he dropped me off, and I can make out Mom in the passenger seat, waving at me. I run the rest of the way, and Mom flings open the door, ushering me in.

"Wow, check *you* out," Mom says, giving me the once-over. "Looks like it was a good party. Did you find Winston?"

"I did." I pat my backpack. "He's in here."

"So, you had fun after all?" Dad asks as I buckle up.

"I want every detail," Mom says, smoothing out my hair. "I mean, look at the state of you. It looks like you danced pretty hardcore in there."

I don't answer; instead, I rest my head against her shoulder, breathing in her orange blossom perfume. As we pull away, Dad turns up his music, and from my window I watch the twisted banner blow away toward the sea.

CHAPTER 13

It's strange having a secret. I've never really had friends I
trust enough to confide in, let alone a pair of track stars who
helped me thwart an evil sea demon that I somehow sum-
moned (still not sure *how* that happened, by the way).

All day Saturday, Quinn and Mike are regular fixtures
on my phone, sending me messages in our group chat that
Mike randomly named Operation Ghost Hunter. I've never
been part of a group chat before, and I'm not used to the
constant buzz in my pocket.

"Someone's popular," Dad says at breakfast, after about
the fifteenth notification.

I roll my eyes, trying to play it cool, but honestly, it's fun
being part of a group.

Quinn: Marion, tell Mike I won the bet.

Mike: No way. You can't win a bet I don't even remember.

I send back a laughing emoji. They've been bickering about this since last night. When we all got home from the dance, they called me in a video chat. Quinn filled in a still-dazed Mike about what happened with Winston. To my surprise, Mike believed every word we told him about Winston, right down to the black ink and pointy tongue. Now he's even trying to take full credit for Winston's demise.

So, I'm basically a hero. That's what you're saying, right? Mike writes.

How do you figure? Quinn writes back. **You were frozen.**

Self-sacrifice!

It's so weird that you don't remember anything, Quinn tells him.

It's hazy, he admits. **And the bits I do remember feel like a dream.**

I'm sorry I got you inked, I tell him. Then I brace myself, waiting for him to say that he doesn't want to be friends anymore.

Wasn't your fault, Quinn interjects.

It kind of sounds like it was, Mike writes. I feel a catch in my throat, but before I can respond, he sends back a slew of laughing-face emojis. **I'm just playing. We're good.**

Stop messing with Marion, Quinn scolds. **You're trying to distract us.**

Distract you from WHAT, Parker?

The fact that you lost the bet! she tells him.

Nope, he argues.

You both won, I type in between bites of Mom's homemade pumpkin scones.

No such thing as ties, Mike says.

I snort out loud. **Last night there was!**

Don't worry, Mike, Quinn writes. **Next time, I'm sure you'll lose fair and square.**

HA! Mike sends another laughing face. **There better not BE a next time. Haven't we vanquished all the demons in South Haven? How many more can there be?**

Who knows? Quinn asks. **Sometimes I still dream about Sarah Goodie.**

Who's Sarah? I ask, adding some sugar to my coffee.

NO ONE WORTH MENTIONING, Mike types in all caps.

It's cool, Mike. She should know, Quinn tells him. **She was Bea's mother. The original witch who cursed South Haven. She tried to drown me in the pond by my house.**

Yeah, but I saved her, Mike says.

Quinn sends back a giant red heart. **You did.**

I freeze, mid-bite, staring at my screen. **Are you guys serious?**

Very serious, Quinn writes. **That's why you should join our group. Like, officially.**

Then we've got to initiate her, Mike says.

I gulp. **What do I have to do to be initiated?**

Mike sends back a milkshake emoji. **Harvey's,** he writes. **After school on Monday. First round's on you. Cool?**

I smile. **Cool.**

"Earth to Marion," Dad says, waving a scone in front of my face.

"What? Sorry." I put my phone down and look across the table. My family stares back at me with tiny smirks on their faces.

"I was just asking if you wanted to go to the bookstore later with me and Margot," Dad says.

"Sure," I tell him, before tearing into the scone with my teeth. "Sounds fun."

Mom eyes us over her coffee mug. "One book each."

Dad frowns. "But—"

"One. Book. Each." She raises her eyebrows in a *don't mess with me* way.

Dad holds up his hands. "Fine. One book each. Got it."

"Seriously," Mom tells him. "We don't have room."

"I got it, I got it." He leans over and kisses her on the cheek, causing her to smile.

Margot rolls her eyes and gets up. "I'm going to take a shower," she says, before floating out of the room.

"And I've got to get ready for work," Mom says with a sigh. "Wedding party today. Wish me luck."

"You got this, babe," Dad tells her, before stealing another scone.

I'm debating having my own second helping as a text comes through on my phone. I'm expecting it to be Quinn and Mike again, but instead, it's Tyler.

Just wanted to say I'm sorry again, he writes. **Are we cool?**

Last night still feels raw; I don't know how to feel about what Tyler did and didn't do. So, I swipe away the message without responding.

Mom leaves about an hour later. We say goodbye, before piling into Dad's truck. Margot gets the front seat, and she spends the first five minutes arguing with him about which song to play. Eventually they agree on Siouxsie and the Banshees, and then we're off.

We drive through South Haven with the windows down, soaking in the autumnal breeze. The remnants of last night's storm are evident all through South Haven: rubber bats and cheesecloth ghosts have fallen from the trees and now lay scattered across leaf-covered lawns. The eyes of jack-o'-lanterns have been made larger by hungry squirrels and chipmunks. Everything looks just a little more menacing, even though the danger is (hopefully) gone.

I settle back and try to enjoy the ride as Margot and Dad sing in the front seat. It isn't long before we arrive in Valport, the next town over from South Haven. A new bookstore opened in the downtown area a few months ago, and it's become Dad and Margot's favorite place. It's called DJ's. The building is one of many in a strip of shops, right across from the main street gazebo. The outside of the store is made of brick and large windows. The inside kind of looks like an old-school living room, with paisley-print carpet, dark wooden shelves, and faded paintings on the walls. In the back, they sell coffee, tea, and hot apple cider.

"After you," Dad says, opening the door for Margot and me. Then he follows us inside.

"OK, you heard your mother. One book each," he reminds us. "No stacks this time." He wrinkles his nose as if he doesn't agree with this restriction. "Meet you at the register in twenty minutes?"

"Thirty," Margot says.

"Deal." He smiles. "Happy shopping, girls." Then he makes his way over to the music section of the store.

Margot salutes his back before turning on her Mary Janes and bounding up the stairs. I know where she's heading: to the literary fiction.

I sigh. Normally, I'd head off to the horror shelves and look at all of the colorful artwork on the covers. But I'm not in the mood to be inspired today. I've had enough of monsters for the time being.

My phone buzzes in my pocket. It's Tyler again.

Marion? Can we talk?

My stomach flutters as I swipe the message away. I'm still not ready to deal with Tyler. I need more time.

Instead, I move toward the botany section. How scary can plants be? I start flipping through one at random, when someone taps me on the shoulder. I turn around, expecting to find Margot or Dad. But it's neither of them. It's Janae and Shannon from school.

"Oh, hey," I say, not covering up my surprise.

They smile at me.

"Hey, Marion," Janae says. "Did you just get here?"

I nod. "My dad and sister are around somewhere."

"Shannon slept over last night, and my mom needed a new book," Janae explains.

"How was the dance?" Shannon asks. "Everyone's saying it was a disaster." Her eyes glitter at the gossip.

I swallow. "What are people saying?"

She shrugs. "Just that the storm really messed things up. The power went out, the hall flooded."

"Did the sprinklers really go off?" Janae asks. "Did it ruin all of your makeups?"

"They were OK," I told them, shifting my weight and looking down at my boots.

"Now I kind of wish we went," Shannon says with a laugh. "Sounds exciting!"

"That's one word for it," I mumble. Then I quickly change the subject. "How was your game?"

At this, they both grin. "You would have loved it," Janae says. "We did a monster version with all of the classics: Frankenstein, Wolf Man, the Creature from the Black Lagoon . . ." She trails off, waving her hands in the air, her bracelets clinking against one another. "You should totally come next time! You would love it."

Shannon gasps and tugs on my arm. "Oh my gosh, she's right. Please come!"

I look at my wrist, wanting to snap the rubber band that's no longer there. I haven't replaced it from last night, and to be honest, I'm not totally sure that I want to. I'm going to talk to Dr. Magesh about it at our next meeting.

"We can even create a special character for you," Janae continues. "Marion the Monster Slayer!"

"Umm," I start.

"OK, you have to do it now. It's like your calling, Mar. You would make *the best* slayer," Shannon says.

"What do you say?" Janae asks, raising one eyebrow hopefully.

I take a deep breath. *Four . . . three . . . two . . .* "Are you sure you want me there?" I ask. "I mean, you never really wanted me to play before."

Janae laughs out loud. "That's not true! We used to invite you all the time, remember? But you always said no, so we just thought you weren't interested."

"Are you sure I won't just ruin your game?" I press. "Because I don't know how to play. And, like, you all have been playing together forever . . ." I trail off, feeling more self-conscious with every word.

"That's why sometimes it's boring. We know each other *too* well at this point," Janae says. "No offense, Shannon."

Shannon shrugs. "None taken."

"Anyway," Janae continues, "we need some fresh blood— someone cool."

"Like *you*!" Shannon says, pointing to my chest.

I blush. "I guess one game can't hurt, right?" I say, surprising myself.

She grins. "You'll be hooked. Trust me. You'll be a D&D lifer by the time you're done."

I smile back. "Don't count on it." But it feels good to be wanted. I don't know why I never appreciated the feeling before.

"I'm adding you to our group chat," Shannon says, taking out her phone. "What's your info?"

After hesitating for a second, I give it to her. She swipes and types, and a moment later, I feel a buzz in my pocket. When I look at the screen, Tanya is already typing a message.

Tanya: YAY! Marion's here! Now we can convince her to do the play with us, too.

Janae laughs. "Uh-oh. She's going to blow up your phone. You'll have to do the play just to get her to stop asking."

I shake my head. "I actually think I'm taking a break from monster-making."

Their jaws drop. "What?" they cry in unison.

"You can't quit," Shannon insists. "You're too good!"

"Everyone's posting about you online," Janae adds. "About how your makeups were the highlight of the dance."

A warmth rolls over me. "Really?"

"Really."

"At least think about it," Janae says, smiling. "I mean, we're just going to keep bugging you."

"You're going to do it," Shannon says. "I can *feel* it!"

I laugh and shake my head again. "Feel what you want, but I'm out."

"Not taking *no* for an answer," Shannon says. "Come on, Janae. Let's leave quickly before she changes her mind."

"Wait, I never said *yes!*" I counter, but they're already giggling and scurrying away.

"Text us later," Janae calls over her shoulder. And then they're both gone.

I remain in place for a while, hovering in front of the botany books, trying to process what just happened.

"You choose one yet?" Margot asks, suddenly appearing in front of me.

She shifts her weight, adjusting the stack of paperbacks under her arm. I eye them.

"What happened to one book?" I ask.

"Mom said one book *each*." She holds up three. "This one's for me. This one is for Mom."

I roll my eyes. "Mom's, huh?"

"Yup. And this one's yours," she says, pulling out a paperback with two teenagers kissing on the cover; one of them has translucent skin.

"Eww, as if I'd read a love story about ghosts."

"Well, are you getting any of those?" She nods to the shelf in front of me.

"No."

"So, this one can be yours then. I'll just borrow it from time to time." She smirks at me before turning on her heels. "Come on. Dad's probably waiting."

Dad *is* waiting by the register as promised, carrying his own stack of books.

"Am I the only one who follows the rules around here?" I ask.

"What?" he asks innocently. "They're for the book club."

"For the book club," Margot repeats.

Dad leans in toward me. "Don't tell your mother and I'll buy you each an extra-large caramel apple cider."

"Fine," I mumble, knowing full well that Dad can't lie *or* keep a secret; he'll show Mom his latest stack of books as soon as she gets home.

He pays and then hands Margot the bag to carry so that he can drape an arm around each of our shoulders as we head out.

CHAPTER 14

By the time that Mom gets home, it's early evening. She kicks off her heels and sighs. Her eyes go straight to the stack of new books on the counter.

"What do we have here?" she asks.

"Margot, you were supposed to bring them upstairs," Dad scolds. He shakes his head, pretending to be disappointed. "Amateur."

"Sorry," Margot tells him, even though she's laughing.

"Quick, I'll distract your mother. Run!" Dad cries, before pulling Mom into a giant bear hug.

Margot grabs the books and darts out of the kitchen. Mom starts tickling Dad in the ribs to get him to let go. Then she turns to me.

"Weren't you watching them?" she teases. "I thought you were the responsible one."

"I was bribed with cider," I confess.

Mom purses her lips. "At least tell me it was caramel, right? Because that I can understand."

"*Obviously,* I got her caramel," Dad tells her. "What kind of monster do you take me for?"

Mom laughs and shrugs out of her coat. "You're still not off the hook. As penance, you and Margot have to cook dinner."

Dad sighs. "I can accept that punishment. *Mar-got!*" he yells up the stairs. "Come back down. We've got dinner duty." He then points a wooden spoon at Mom and me. "My sous-chef will be here shortly. You two, out!" He ushers us out of the kitchen, following us into the living room. There, he drops the act. I catch him giving Mom a tender kiss on the forehead.

"We'll let you know when the food's ready," he says.

"Thanks," she tells him with a smile.

Dad goes back to the kitchen, joined by a reluctant Margot. We hear them bickering about what to cook.

Mom giggles and stretches out on the couch. "Come sit with me."

I grab my sketchbook and a pencil from off the end table. Then I collapse beside her, breathing in her familiar orange blossom scent. She flicks on the TV as I begin to draw. My phone starts buzzing in my pocket. I place my pad down and glance at the screen. It's a slew of new messages from my lunch table chat.

Tanya: MARION! Have you thought about the play?

Janae: Are you gonna do it?

Shannon: She's gonna do it.

The three of them send a stream of GIFs, all with Audrey II, the monstrous plant from the play.

Mom's eyes are still on the TV, but she's smiling. She doesn't ask what's going on, but her look makes me feel like I should explain anyway.

"It's just some kids from my lunch table," I tell her as the phone continues to buzz in my hand. "They're trying to get me to do the play."

Mom turns to me. "You said yes, right?"

I tighten my grip on my phone. "No. I'm taking a break from monsters, I think."

"No, you're not," Mom says. "I mean, look what you're drawing." She motions to my notebook.

I follow her gaze to the picture, which is a rough sketch of Sarah Goodie, the pond witch Quinn told me about this morning. Her teeth are jagged, her eyes hollow, her hair floating around her like black snakes.

"She's looking pretty monstrous to me," Mom says pointedly.

I cover the page with my hand. "This is different."

"Really?" She arches one of her dark brows and sits up straighter. "Baby, listen. Monsters can be scary, but they can also teach us how to be brave."

"What do you mean?" I ask.

"Doesn't monster-making help you feel less anxious?"

"I guess," I admit. "Most of the time." *Except at the dance...*

She reaches out and twirls a lock of my hair. My phone is still vibrating with new messages that I haven't read yet.

"It looks like your friends *really* want you to do the play," Mom says.

"It's just because I'm the only makeup artist at school," I mumble.

Mom snatches my phone from my hands.

"Hey!"

"Calm down, I'm just googling something." Her manicured fingers swipe against the screen for a moment. I peer over her shoulder to see what she's searching for.

"There's an Audrey II costume on sale for $49.95 at Party Town." She tosses my phone back. "They don't want you in the play just because you're good at makeup—even though you are *incredibly* good at makeup." She places a cool hand on my cheek. "They can buy a premade costume anywhere. They want you to be part of the play because they like *you*. Not just because you're talented, but because you're sweet. And smart. And fun."

I feel myself blushing as I wriggle out of her grasp. "That's not true."

Mom glances at my phone as more messages come through. "I think it is," she says. "And I think you should tell them you're in."

"It's not that easy, Mom. I can't just talk to people. I'm not good at it. What if they get sick of me? I'm not like you."

"Not like me?" Mom blinks. "What's that supposed to mean?"

"You're—I don't know . . ." I search for the right word. "*Popular*. Everyone loves you. You've got like a million followers on social media."

At this, Mom laughs. "Oh, honey. That's not real life. Who cares about social media?"

I don't answer. Mom stops laughing. She reaches for my hair again, and for a moment, we sit together in silence as she weaves the thick strands through her fingers.

"I was just like you growing up, you know," she finally says. "Shy. Anxious. I used to throw up before class presentations."

"Seriously?"

"Seriously. It took me forever to find my voice, and even longer to find my confidence."

"Yeah, right," I snort.

"It's true! You've already got so many strategies, more than I had at your age. I didn't figure out how to manage my anxiety symptoms until I was in my twenties. And by then, I'd missed out on so much."

I turn to face her. "Like what?"

"Like almost everything: dances, parties, jobs, internships, you name it." She leans in close, our foreheads practically touching. "Take a chance, Marion. Surprise yourself."

Before I can answer, my phone buzzes again. Mom smiles and leans back to watch the TV, pretending to give me privacy as I open my messages. It's more of the same, them telling me how much fun we'll have together if I do the play. Maybe they're right. Maybe Mom's right—maybe it'll be fun.

But how can I be sure that making another monster is safe?

There are only two people who know the truth about last night. I open my other chat with Quinn and Mike. I've never asked a friend for advice before. But I guess there's a first time for everything.

Me: Can I ask you something?

Quinn: Of course.

Mike: No.

Quinn: MIKE!

Mike: Kidding. What's up, M?

Me: Mrs. Anderson asked me to do the makeup for the school play. Do you think I should?

Quinn: Why not? You'd do a great plant monster.

Mike: Maybe TOO good.

Me: That's kind of what I'm afraid of . . .

Quinn: You don't have to worry about a repeat of Winston. That wouldn't have happened without the eclipse.

Me: You sure?

Mike: She THINKS she's sure.

Quinn: I'm VERY sure.

Me: So you think I should do it?

At this, they both type back **YES!**

Is this what friendship is? Taking a risk? Trusting people?

Before I type my answer to my other group, another message comes in.

Mike: Speaking of monsters, Tyler keeps texting me.

Me: WHAT?

Mike: He says you've been ignoring him. Can't you at least text him back?

Me: I don't want to talk to him.

Mike: But it wasn't his fault. He was possessed!

Quinn: I hate to say it, but Mike's right.

Mike: I'M ALWAYS RIGHT, PARKER!

Quinn ignores him, though. Instead, she writes: **At least see what he has to say, Mar.**

I nod, even though she can't see me.

Take a risk, I tell myself. *Trust your friends.*

I take a deep breath before opening the last message from Tyler.

Hey, I type.

Tyler responds a second later, sending me a smiley face. **Hey.**

CHAPTER 15

The next morning, I wake up to the scent of pumpkin spice and cinnamon: Mom must be making a pie. I follow my nose to the kitchen, drifting through the house in my pajamas.

"Uh-uh," Mom tells me, waggling a finger. She's wearing her apron, and there are patches of flour mixed in with the printed cherries. "This is for your company. Have something else for breakfast."

Margot shuffles in a few seconds after me. "What company?"

"Marion has a friend coming over after dinner," Mom explains, making an obvious effort to keep her face neutral.

Margot goes for the pie, but Mom pushes it away. Instead, Margot reaches for the coffee.

"Which friend?" she asks.

"Tyler," I admit.

At this, she frowns. "Didn't he steal your mask?"

"It was just a misunderstanding," Mom says, saving me from having to explain. "Here, honey, I think I have some scones left, if you want." She leads Margot to the table, holding up a tray of leftover baked goods.

I lean against the counter, thinking about last night. Tyler asked if we could reschedule our movie marathon so that he could apologize in person. I wanted to do it, but Mom said no to the marathon.

"You have school tomorrow," she reminded me.

So instead, I suggested one movie to Tyler. He agreed, sending me about a million thumbs-up.

Today, though, I'm nervous. What if I can't help it, and I'm still mad at him, even after he apologizes? What if he's annoying? Or worse, what happens if he decides *I'm* annoying, and that he doesn't like me anymore?

At least now I have Quinn and Mike to talk to about this kind of stuff.

"Morning, everyone," Dad says, stretching in the doorway. "Oooh, pie!"

"That's for later," Mom tells him.

He slumps into a chair, sulking until Mom hands him a scone.

"Marion, did you tell everyone the news?" Mom asks, in between sips of coffee.

"What news?" Dad asks.

"I'm going to do the makeup for the school play," I tell him. My stomach does a little flip; saying the words out loud somehow makes the decision feel more real.

Dad fist-bumps the air in an exaggerated way. "That's my girl!"

Even Margot smiles. "Guess I'll have to break my vow and set foot in that horrible middle school again."

"You'll come see it?" I ask.

"Obviously."

Mom squeals. "I'm so excited! You're going to kill it, baby."

"I hope so," I mumble, but it does feel good to see them so excited about something I'm a part of.

Though their excitement doesn't hold a candle to that of my lunch table friends. When I texted them the news, they sent me video messages of themselves dancing and screaming. I stared at my phone in disbelief. Mom was right: I *was* wanted. Now I just have to tell Mrs. Anderson in school tomorrow. The play itself isn't for a few months still, so maybe by then I'll feel ready to sculpt another monster. Until then, I'm going to stick with pen and paper.

I grab my notebook from off the shelf and spend the rest of the morning sketching on the kitchen table as my family bustles around. I try out a few different things, but I keep coming back to the drawing from last night—the one of Sarah Goodie. There's something familiar about her even though I've never seen her face.

I outline the sketch in black, coloring her dark hair that floats around her like tentacles. Then I start shading in her black eyes, her evil smile. I add a dress that floats in the water, resembling seaweed. Using a green pencil, I add in some color.

"She looks wicked," Margot says, leaning over my shoulder.

"Thanks," I say, pleased.

"I've got to go to the library to return a few books," she says. "Want to come for the walk?"

Margot never asks me to go anywhere with her, so I jump at the opportunity. Maybe the walk will take my mind off Tyler coming over in just a few hours.

I put away my art supplies, and we head out. We don't talk much as we walk, but the sun feels good on my face, especially after last night's storm.

When we get home, I help Mom make dinner. After we eat, I run up to my room to change, but I get distracted by my workshop. When I got home the other night, I threw Winston in one of my desk drawers and locked it, before jumping on the video chat with Quinn and Mike. Now, though, with Tyler coming over, I feel the need to check on Winston.

Slowly, I take out the little key and fit it into the lock, opening the metal drawer. Even though I know what to expect, I gasp at the sight of my monster, lying dormant in the shadows. He's lifeless, just a husk, but I still reach out and touch the edges, the eyeholes, the hollow mouth—just to make sure. Satisfied, I lock him back inside.

Then I shift into cleaning mode, methodically putting my tools back in their jars and screwing on the lids. I use alcohol to rub down the airbrush, and I drag a Wet One across the surface of the table.

"Hey, honey," Mom says, appearing in the doorway. "Cleaning up?"

"You can say that."

She nods, looking around. "Where's Winston? I thought he'd be out on display, front and center?"

"I don't feel like seeing him right now," I admit, tossing the wipe into the trash.

The doorbell rings.

"Wait—what time is it?" I ask, grabbing for my phone with my ink-stained fingers. "That must be Tyler! Mom, why did you let me stay up here for so long?" My heart begins to race.

"Don't worry," Mom says. "I'll have your father entertain him until you're ready."

"Mom—no!"

"Kidding! I'll go save him. You get changed." She turns and trots down the stairs, the sound of her heels snapping against the hardwood floors.

Quickly, I turn off the light to my workshop and slip into my bedroom. The mirror hanging above my desk shows a girl with a crooked bun and ink-stained tights. I yank my hair free, give it a shake, and swap out my skirt for a pair of fitted black jeans and a T-shirt.

"What? No flannel today?" I hear Dad ask from downstairs.

Mom must be failing; I need to save Tyler myself. I drop my dirty clothes into the laundry basket before flying down the stairs, my fingers getting caught in the spiderwebs on the banister that we've yet to take down.

Tyler is sitting on the couch politely drinking a glass of apple cider as Dad flicks through his vinyl collection.

"That's not punk," Dad is saying, throwing shade at Tyler's Clash T-shirt. "This"—he holds up a Minor Threat record—"is punk."

"Dad, seriously?" I ask, making my way around the coffee table. "Tyler doesn't need a music lesson." I smile shyly at Tyler, tucking my hair behind my ears. "Hey."

He grins back at me, causing my cheeks to burn. "Hey."

Dad looks between the two of us and shakes his head before punching the ON button with his thumb.

The heavy bass and fast-paced guitar riffs fill the room, and Dad starts bopping around in the most embarrassing way. "Real punk," he tells Tyler.

Tyler nods his head in time to the beat. "Sounds good, Mr. Jones," he says loudly to be heard over the music.

"Dad, come on!"

At this, Mom makes her way into the room, flicking the stereo off. She raises an eyebrow at Dad. "Leave the kids alone, honey."

Dad smiles at her. "What? It was just a little bit of music education."

"I like it, Mr. Jones," Tyler says, and he sounds sincere enough that I don't even think he's lying just to impress my dad.

"Of course you do. It's actually good, unlike that garbage band you have on your shirt."

"Dad!"

Mom tugs on his sleeve. "Come on, honey. I'm sure they'd rather watch their movie than your dancing."

Dad stalls in front of the TV. "What movie are you watching? Do you want *Cujo*? I still have it on streaming if you want—"

"Hey," Margot says, appearing in the doorway. She looks from me to Dad and Tyler and back again. A smirk creeps across her lips. "You must be Tyler."

"That's me," Tyler says, looking nervous all over again.

I shoot her a pleading look, before making eyes at Dad. Thankfully, she gets the hint.

"Come on, Dad," she says, patting him on the back. "I haven't beaten you at basketball in a while."

This gets him. "It's been approximately thirteen months and twenty-eight days since you last played ball with me."

"Honey, don't be so dramatic," Mom tells him.

"Yeah, let's go before I change my mind," Margot says.

Mom smiles. "Whoever wins will get first dibs on the pie."

"Oh, it's on!" He points at Margot. "That pie is *mine*."

"You wish, old man."

"Hey, who you calling old?"

I mouth the words *thank you* to my sister as she steers Dad out of the living room. Mom flashes me a look before returning to the kitchen, finally leaving Tyler and me alone.

"Sorry about them," I say, twisting the bottom of my shirt; my hands don't seem to know what to do anymore without my rubber band. "My dad's just—I don't know. He's just kind of weird."

Tyler smiles. "No, your parents are cool. I told you—they're way cooler than mine."

There's a beat of silence between us. I debate throwing the movie on, but no—not yet. He came here to say something, and neither of us is going to relax until he says it.

"So," he starts.

"So . . ."

His face reddens, and he rubs at his cheeks with the palms of his hand. "I'm sorry," he starts. "I'm just really nervous."

"It's OK," I tell him.

"No, it's definitely not OK. I swear I didn't mean to steal from you." He drops his hands in front of him and begins wringing them together. "I don't know what came over me. It was like I was possessed or something. All of a sudden, the mask was in my hands, and then I put it on at the dance, and then the storm started, and then I can't really remember . . ." He trails off, his skin growing redder with each breath.

"I'm sorry, too," I say, feeling lighter as I say the words; I've been holding them in since first laying eyes on Winston at the dance.

"What do *you* have to be sorry for?" Tyler asks.

"I don't know. Let's just forget it all, OK?" I glance at him hopefully. "Restart?"

He grins, relief flooding his face "Restart."

I grab the remote, aiming it at the TV. "Which movie do you want to watch?" I ask, scrolling through my saved films. "*The Thing, Pumpkinhead . . .*"

"Hey, there's *Gremlins*," Tyler says, pointing to the screen. "Definitely *Gremlins*. I mean, it's a cinematic classic."

I roll my eyes. "If you say so."

I hit PLAY and sit near Tyler as the movie starts, leaving an entire couch cushion between us. Even so, I'm very aware of my posture and my breathing and the rate at which my heart is racing.

The movie opens with a man wandering through the city to find a present for his son. He ends up buying a cute little furry creature called a *mogwai*, which (spoiler alert) has the ability to multiply and turn into these violent little gremlins. But about five minutes in, the camera shifts to a snow-covered town, decorated in red bows and wreaths.

"I told you this was a Christmas movie!" I cry.

"It's *so* much more than a Christmas movie," Tyler says.

I make a face at the screen. "It's too cute for Halloween."

Tyler's eyes suddenly widen. "Halloween! Hey, that reminds me . . ." He fumbles in his pocket for his phone. "I never got to interview you. Would you be up for it now? The article is going to be on the cover."

"The cover?" I gasp.

"Yup. I even have the headline already: *Marion Jones Makes Monsters and Magic*. What do you think?"

I don't have any words, so instead, I just nod.

He holds out his phone. "Is it cool if I record you talking?"

"OK," I tell him. *Three, two, one . . .*

"Don't worry, it'll be a piece of cake." He smiles at me, then presses RECORD. "Marion Jones interview,

November second," he says into the phone. Then he turns to me. "When did you start doing makeup?"

"I guess when I was five," I tell him, thinking back. "My mom helped me make my own costume for Halloween. And I did the makeup myself."

"What were you?"

"A vampire."

"Was it any good?"

I snort. "I was five. What do you think?"

He giggles. "OK, next question. What do you love about makeup?"

Everything, I want to say. "The creativity. The freedom." I hope that didn't sound too cheesy, but Tyler continues to nod as if I just said the most interesting thing in the world. After Friday, I didn't think I'd ever want anything to do with makeup again. But Mom must be right—or at least kind of right. Because even though one of my creations came to life, I still can't imagine my life without makeup.

"How did you start doing makeup for the school dances?" Tyler asks, moving on to the next question.

This one makes me smile. "I used to make fake blood for other kids in the neighborhood when we were in elementary school. I'd paint on wounds with gelatin and food coloring, and they'd go home and gross out their parents."

Tyler laughs. "So, you were really popular with the PTO, huh?"

"Yeah, I didn't get invited to many playdates. I've always been kind of a loner." *Why am I telling him this?* I clear my throat. "But anyway, I guess it started with that. Then trick-or-treaters would ask me to do their makeup, and that kind of just evolved."

The longer we talk, the more comfortable I feel answering his questions. At a certain point, I lose track of which questions are for the paper and which questions are just for Tyler's curiosity. It feels nice, though, talking about my craft.

Finally, he hits the RECORD button again, turning it off. "I think I got what I needed," he tells me. "Not bad, right?"

"Not at all," I admit.

"Oh, one more thing. I wanted to include pictures of your makeup, but everything got kind of messed up because of the storm. I was wondering if I could use the one you took of me before the dance." He shows me a photo on his phone—the one I sent him—and there Winston is: his head resting on the shoulders of a boy wearing red flannel and black jeans, his arms poised above his head as if to imitate a real-life monster.

I nearly fall off the couch.

Tyler blinks. "Did I do something wrong?"

I shake my head. "No, sorry."

His words make me suddenly very conscious of my tight shoulders, raised so high that they practically reach my earlobes. I try to relax them down, settling my back into the couch. From the corner of my eye, I see Tyler tuck his phone back into his pocket, his head bowed sheepishly. My stomach turns as I think that I've upset him. How do I tell him that I just can't see him wearing Winston's mask again, in a picture or in real life?

"Thank you," I finally say. "I mean, it's pretty amazing that you got me on the cover."

"It's not a big deal," he says quietly.

For a moment, we both just watch the movie, and I can hear every breath he takes, along with the ticking of Mom's cuckoo clock hanging on the far wall across the room.

We can't go on for the whole movie like this, I think. *At this rate, Tyler's going to leave before it's even over.*

I scooch a little bit closer to him, close enough so that I can smell the clean scent of his shampoo when he turns his head, close enough so that the sides of our arms and knees make contact. Tyler's eyes widen in surprise, and now he's the one who looks stiff, his posture perfectly upright, as if he doesn't know what to do with his hands. I search his eyes for any sign of yellow or serpent—for a sign of Winston. But to my relief, it's just Tyler.

I smile, and he smiles back.

"When do they turn into gremlins?" I ask, nodding at the screen.

"Pretty soon," he says. "Billy's going to accidentally feed the mogwai after midnight, and then they'll transform. You might actually like that scene—it's pretty gruesome."

"I still think it's too cutesy to be really gruesome. I mean, I wouldn't call this a horror movie."

Tyler shrugs. "I was pretty scared the first time I watched it."

"How old were you? Five?" I tease.

He smiles. "Funny."

The tension seems to have lifted, and I continue to tease him until the smell of cinnamon and nutmeg fills the room, and Mom comes parading in with two pieces of her famous pumpkin pie, complete with dollops of homemade whipped cream.

"Snack time," she says cheerfully, handing us each a plate and a fork. "If you eat it quickly enough, you *may* get to have seconds before your father devours the rest of it." She winks at me before turning to the TV. "What movie is this?" She squints. "*Gremlins*? Are you kidding? This isn't even a Halloween movie."

I burst out laughing and point my fork at Tyler. "See?"

Tyler just shakes his head. "Haters . . ."

Mom flashes me a smile before returning to the kitchen, where she, no doubt, pretends to do other things besides eavesdropping on Tyler and me.

I turn to my pie and take a heavenly bite, savoring the spice and the cream, and the graham cracker shortbread crust that Grandma Goldie perfected in her Californian bakery. When I look back up, I notice that Tyler is just staring at his slice.

"What's the matter? Do you not like pumpkin? Or pie?" I ask. "Because I don't think we can be friends if you don't like pie."

He laughs. "No, I love pumpkin pie. It just looks too perfect to eat."

I raise an eyebrow. "Are you being serious?"

"Kind of."

"Just eat it. The cream is going to melt." I take another large bite and close my eyes as I chew. "It's *so* good."

When I open my eyes, Tyler is scooping the tiniest amount onto his fork. "Oh, come on. Get in there." I grab his fork out of his hand, shovel a large amount on top, then hand it back to him. "Bon appétit."

Tyler doesn't hesitate and swallows the entire forkful. "This is brilliant."

"Right?"

"If your mom handed me this slice and told me that eating it would turn me into a gremlin, I would be like, *OK. I guess I'm a gremlin now.* It'd be worth it."

"So, you'd trade your humanity for a dessert?"

"In a heartbeat."

I take another bite, and a for a moment we sit side by side enjoying our pie, not speaking, but this time the silence doesn't feel uncomfortable; it feels peaceful. We both start to relax and get lost in the movie, making commentary as it rolls, adding extra dialogue and funny lines. By the time the last evil gremlin gets melted by the sun into a slimy blob—which I have to admit, *is* a pretty cool special effects scene—our plates are empty, as is the candy bowl in front of us. And I've forgotten to be nervous while sitting this close to Tyler.

I'm so comfortable that I almost don't notice the *Gremlins* theme song kicking in as the credits start to roll.

"Aww, man. This song has been stuck in my head since Halloween," Tyler says. "I even dreamt about it. Twice!" He launches into his own rendition of the song, scrunching up his face as he pretends to jam on an imaginary keyboard.

I place my hand on his arm. "You should stop before you hurt yourself." I then reach for the remote control, snapping the movie into silence.

"Hey, why'd you turn it off? I was just getting to the good part."

I raise an eyebrow. "*What* good part?"

He grins. "Admit it: you liked the movie."

I shrug, trying my hardest to look casual. "I didn't hate it," I admit. "But I still say it's a Christmas movie."

"OK, fine, maybe it was a little more Christmassy than

I remembered. Let's compromise and call it a genre-bender. You know, like *The Nightmare Before Christmas*."

"Oh, I love that movie."

"Same! Want to watch it now?"

"I wish, but I don't think my mom will let us. It's a school night, remember? But maybe next time."

"Yeah, I guess you're right." He stands up and stretches his legs, still bopping his head and humming the *Gremlins* theme song as he puts on his jacket.

"You're never going to get that song out of your head if you keep humming it," I warn.

"I can't help it—it's like stuck on repeat. Oh, and this other one." He immediately switches tunes, instead whistling the opening bars of "Somebody's Watching Me" by Rockwell.

"You know it?" he asks in between notes.

My knuckles whiten as I grip the remote control. For a moment, I don't answer; I simply listen to Tyler sing the familiar tune that had nearly drowned us two nights ago.

"Yeah, I kind of know it," I say quietly.

I look over at his face, at his brown eyes, at the way his lips move. *Ten . . . nine . . . eight . . .* I find myself searching his skin for leftover scales, for a flapping gill, or a slippery black tongue.

But the more I stare, the more I start to smile, because there's nothing monstrous about the boy in front of me. It's just Tyler. *Real* Tyler. The guy who can't draw to save his life but is the best writer on the school paper; the guy with the goofy smile and wild hair; the guy who held my hand and asked me on my first date to watch a monster movie together.

Is this a date?

My stomach flips as he looks back at me, but for once it feels like a good flip.

"Come *on*, Marion!" he cries. "Sing with me!"

At first, the shyness burns, but Tyler seems so incredibly free—not caring a lick about his off-key voice or how silly he looks as he bops around in my living room.

And so, with one deep breath, I join in, singing along at the top of my lungs, not worrying about how I sound, or who else hears (my mom, probably giggling in the kitchen).

The entire moment feels like an ending to our own 1980s horror movie: Girl creates Monster. Girl meets Boy. Boy turns into Monster. Girl defeats Monster. Girl and Boy become friends ...

And just like all good eighties movies, ours should end in a freeze-frame, our hands intertwined, punching the air in time to the beat, until just like that, the song fades out, the credits roll, and all that's left are the two of us and our semipermanent smiles.

CHAPTER 16

But that's not exactly where the movie ends. Once we finish the song, Tyler says his dad is here. We make our way to the door, and for a second, he looks like he might try and hug me. But my dad is hovering in the doorway, and his dad is watching from the car.

"See you tomorrow," he says instead.

"Night," I say with a smile.

Tyler leaves, and Dad shuts off the front light after Mr. Dash drives away. Dad stares at me.

"Don't," I beg, rolling my eyes.

"What?" Dad asks innocently. "I didn't say anything."

"Night, Dad." I lean over and kiss him on the cheek.

"No fist bump this time?" he teases.

"Nope. Love you," I call over my shoulder as I climb up the stairs.

"Love you more," he calls back.

Alone in my room, I know I should go to sleep, but my heart is racing too fast. Instead, I put pajamas on and grab my sketchbook. I continue coloring the pond witch until my phone buzzes with a new message. My stomach dips. Maybe it's Tyler.

Quinn: How was your big date?

I laugh and type back, **It wasn't a date.**

Mike: Did he grow fins halfway through the movie?

Me: ☺ Nope. Fin free.

Mike: What are you going to do if he DOES turn back into Winston?

Quinn: Stop it, Mike! Tyler's not going to turn back into a monster.

Me: He doesn't even remember anything. No one does. Isn't that kind of weird?

Mike: Everything in South Haven is weird.

Me: But why are we the only ones who notice?

Quinn: I have a theory.

Mike: Here we go . . .

Quinn: PSYCHICS.

Mike sends back a rolling-eyes emoji. ***What are you talking about, Parker? We can't see into the future.***

No—not that kind of psychic, she explains. ***I'm talking about the sixth sense. You know, the ability to see the supernatural?***

Mike: It was just a coincidence.

Quinn: You call three different monsters in one year a coincidence?

Mike: Maybe.

I stare at my phone and bite down on my bottom lip. In truth, I think Mike *does* believe in the supernatural, no matter how much he tries to deny it. One thing's for sure: I most definitely believe. Even Mom's tarot card reading has a whole new meaning given everything that's happened.

Quinn: There are no such thing as coincidences.

I'm starting to think that, too, I admit.

Quinn: HA! See, Mike?

Mike: Whatever. Can we talk about something else? Something NOT supernatural? I need to go to bed soon.

Quinn: Need to get your beauty sleep?

Mike: You know it.

Quinn sends back a laughing face, then turns the conversation to me. **What are you doing now, Marion?**

Me: Just drawing.

Quinn: Cool. Show us.

Me: My picture??

Quinn: Yeah. Why not?

I don't usually show people my art before it's finished, but admittedly, this is looking pretty cool so far. I snap a photo and send it through the chat. I'm caught off guard when the three dots dance along the screen for what feels like forever. *Oh no. Do they hate it? Do they think I'm a weirdo for drawing something so creepy?*

Finally, Quinn types something. **How did you know what Sarah looks like?**

Me: You described her to me.

Quinn: No I didn't. I just told you she was a witch in the pond and that she tried to drown me.

I lean back against my pillow, trying to remember our conversation about Sarah Goodie. *Didn't she describe her to me?* My eyes flicker from the screen to the drawing and back again.

Quinn: You got her EXACTLY right.

Mike: Don't start, Parker.

Quinn: Come on, Mike!

Mike: Nope. Don't say it.

Say what? What's going on? I bite my lip and wait for an answer.

PSYCHIC, Quinn types again.

I laugh, but then I quickly realize that Quinn's being serious. Mike types the word **STOP,** but Quinn ignores him.

Quinn: There's something bigger going on here. We need to figure out what. What makes us so special? Especially you, Marion.

I'm not special, I write, but my fingers feel tingly as I type.

I remember Mom's tarot reading and her words: *"There's magic in makeup."* What if Quinn's right?

> **Quinn: We need to talk about this in person. Tomorrow after school. At Harvey's. You in?**
>
> **Mike: This is silly.**
>
> **Quinn: You in???**
>
> **Mike: I'm always in.**
>
> **Quinn: What about you, Marion?**

I don't know what's going on in South Haven, or what my role is in it. But I do know one thing: I need to find out. And if I'm going on another adventure, there's no one I'd rather have with me than Quinn and Mike.

Taking a deep breath, I swipe my fingers across the screen, the two words that I'm pretty sure will change my life forever.

I'm in.

ACKNOWLEDGMENTS

This book was one of my favorites to write, and it was also very personal: Marion's anxiety was based off of my own struggles growing up. Like her, I used my art (writing) as a coping strategy. I was a nerdy kid who loved all things spooky, especially cheesy eighties horror movies, with their iconic special effects and monster makeups. I guess you can say that I've had Marion's story in me for a while.

So first and foremost, I'd like to thank everyone at Amulet Books for bringing this book to life, especially Hallie Patterson, Amy Vreeland, Rachael Marks, Deena Fleming, Brann Garvey, Andrew Smith, Jody Mosley, Maggie Lehrman, Megan Evans, Patricia McNamara O'Neill, Jenny Choy, Richard Slovak, and Regina Castillo. Thank you to Jade Rector, Kelley McMorris, and David Coulson for creating such a gorgeously spooky cover!

Extra-special thanks to my editor, Emily Daluga, who I think would be the best monster slayer if she lived in South Haven. (And I'm pretty sure she has actual superpowers.)

Speaking of superpowers, thank you to my agent, Kathleen Rushall, for reading an early draft of this book and saying *YES!*, and for being a voice of reason, creativity, and kindness ever since.

Thank you to my mom, who passed down her love of *Creature from the Black Lagoon*, and my dad, who preferred *Little Shop of Horrors* and *Young Frankenstein*. I used to love our family movie nights, and I tried to add a touch of that here in *Unmasked*.

To my older brother, DJ, I think I've finally turned you into a Halloween convert; welcome to the spooky club. Thanks to the rest of my family: Megan, Kaylee, Zoe, Lex, the Venerusos, the Haydens, and the Hurds. Also sending lots of love to Janice, Dave, Jon, and Philippa.

Of course, thank you to my husband, Chris—love you always—and our children, Ruby and Leo, who give Mommy lots of snuggles, as well as time to write and read and repeat.

Thanks to my friends, my BMS family, my Spooky Middle Grade group, and of course, my Middle Ground Book Fest teammates: Janae Marks, Shannon Doleski, and Tanya Guerrero.

Huge shout-out to Tyler Green, the special effects artist who answered my *millions* of questions about monster-making. Winston definitely wouldn't exist without his help, expertise, and talent.

Last, but certainly not least, a million thanks to you, dear reader. I now dub you as the newest member of Operation Ghost Hunter. Keep your eyes wide open and remember to RUN! (Or in this case, *dance*.)

ABOUT THE AUTHOR

Lorien Lawrence is a writer and middle school English teacher from Connecticut. When she's not buried under a stack of books, she can be found exploring spooky haunts with her family.

READ ALL THE
FRIGHT WATCH
BOOKS — IF YOU DARE!

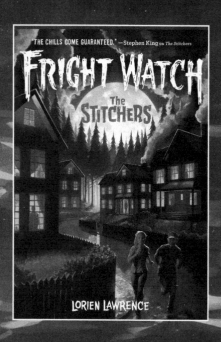

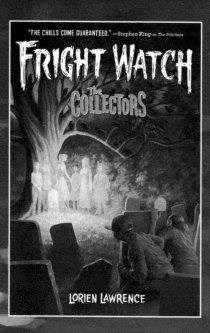